Rhonda,
May God bless
you and may your
life be filled with
friends who are to
Am.

The Opera Ghost Lives

The Red Diamond of Nadirijna

Ann M. Kraft

HIS PUB G
The Publishing Group

www.hispubg.com
A division of HISpecialists, llc

Published by HIS Publishing Group,
a Division of Human Improvement Specialists, llc
Contact: info@hispubg.com

First Printing

All characters in this book are fictitious and any resemblance to real persons, deceased or living is coincidental.

Scriptures are taken from the *King James Version of the Bible*, in the public domain.

Library of Congress Control Number: 2011921579

ISBN: 978-0-615-44520-5

Printed and bound in the United States of America

Dedication

To my sisters Karen and Susan and my brothers John and David; thanks for making my childhood memorable and my life as an adult never dull or boring. Our real life adventures aided my imagination and gave me solid ground on which to build my dreams of being a writer. I love you all very much.

Special thanks to my wonderful husband Curtis and our daughter Emily who continue to encourage me to write. I couldn't do anything without their constant love and support.

Characters

Erik Geraurd is a disfigured man that used to live in the Paris Opera House. He is also known as the Phantom of the Opera or the Opera Ghost.

Amalie Geraurd is the daughter of Gaston Girault. She is a very intelligent woman who helps Erik leave the Paris Opera House. She is now his wife.

Louisa Geraurd is the daughter of Erik and Amalie.

Gaston Girault is the deceased father of Amalie and unlikely friend to Erik that helped him realize that there was more to his life than staying hidden.

Louise Girault is Amalie's deceased mother. Gaston's deceased wife.

Chester Rousseau is Amalie's coachman.

Meg Rousseau is her housekeeper. They are more like family than servants. Chester and Meg are married and they were Gaston's servants that stayed on at the chateau after he died.

Isabel Durand is Chester's and Meg's daughter.

Peter Durand is Isabel's husband and Erik's best friend.

Frederic Rousseau is the deceased son of Chester and Meg.

Anna Rousseau is the widow of Frederic.

The Persian or Daroga is Erik's longtime friend that saved his life from the Shah of Persia.

Darius is the Persian's servant.

Reverend Troudeaux is a longtime friend of the Girault family and is the spiritual leader of the small church in the village of Trie-Chateau.

Contents

Past Lives

*D*arius found that he was in a precarious situation outside the window of the flat that he and his master shared. He had opened the window, quickly setting his feet upon the ledge and closing the window behind him after hearing the angry voices that had entered their living quarters uninvited. He hated that he had left his master to fend off the intruders by himself but being courageous had never been a quality that was prevalent in him. He decided to ease carefully along the ledge of their flat. He kept his back tightly against the facade of the building, careful not to lean forward which may cause him to lose his balance. As he reached the outside of the window of the room his master and the intruders were in, he could hear their voices and what was being said.

Inside, the Persian had been subdued by two very large men wearing attire that he recognized to be that of his former employer, the Shah of Persia. It had been almost twenty-two years since he had been exiled from his homeland for his part in helping Erik escape the death that had been planned for him by the Shah. It was fortunate that a corpse that had been dressed in clothes similar to Erik's was found and was believed to be him. The finding of the body was fortunate for the Persian because it saved him from being imprisoned or worse, executed. Instead he had all of his property stripped from him, along with the loss of the favor of the Royal House and had been exiled never to return to Persia.

He was surprised to find himself in the predicament in which he was currently being held prisoner. He knew of no reasons that the Royal House of Persia would seek him out since he had left with nothing and had never spoken one word to anyone that Erik was still alive at the time the body had washed up onto the shore. He wished to ask his captors why they had come but they didn't allow him to speak. Instead they bound his hands behind him, gagged him and blind-folded his eyes. They proceeded to place him in a chair and beat him with their fists.

After they had finished with their torture and the Persian's face was bloody and swollen, they removed the handkerchief from his mouth and the blindfold but left his hands bound.

The strange man with a scar underneath his left eye walked around him as he spoke. "It has been many years Daroga. I suppose you thought you had gotten away with it after all of these years."

The Persian spit out some blood that had collected in his mouth from the beating he had just received. "Gotten away with what?" he asked as he tried to keep from passing out.

"Don't be daft, Hessam. You know exactly what I'm talking about."

It had been many years since he had heard the name that his mother had bestowed upon him the day he was born. He was usually referred to as Daroga by those that had known his past and Persian by those that he was merely acquainted with for a short period of time. He had only recently revealed his birth name to Amalie since she had grown tired of referring to him as Persian and felt that it was rude to do so when he had a perfectly good name in which she could identify him. He had told her that it meant protector and she thought it was very appropriate in light of what he had done for Erik. However, at this moment it didn't seem all that appropriate being that he wasn't even sure he would be able to protect himself against the men that had entered his home. All he could do now was answer their questions and hope that they would release him.

"I assure you, I don't," insisted Hessam.

With that response the other large man punched him once more in the right jaw and then said, "Did that help you remember Daroga?"

"You can continue to beat me as long as you like and it will produce the same response that I'm giving you now. How is it that you know my name and yet I don't recognize you?" His left eye was swollen shut and blood continued to pool inside his mouth which he spit onto the floor to keep from choking on it.

The man with the scar underneath his eye knelt in front of him and said, "How I know your name is unimportant. Now, if you are done asking your ridiculous questions let's get back to the matter at hand." He rubbed his chin and then walked behind Hessam, putting his hand on his shoulder. "You mean to tell me that you don't remember taking that which was not yours from the treasury room of the Shah?"

He still was not clear on what it was he was to have stolen. He spit one more time and then answered, "I don't remember taking anything from the treasury room. In fact, it is inconceivable that I would've even been able to enter the room without anyone's knowledge. It was guarded heavily if my memory serves me correctly. Anyone leaving was searched thoroughly to assure that nothing had been taken."

"That may be true but then how do you explain the Red Diamond of Nadirijna being missing from its resting place inside the treasury room?"

"The Red Diamond of Nadirijna is missing? How is that possible? It was there two nights before the Shah gave the orders to have all of the workers that built the palace executed. The Shah and I entered the room together and left the room together after we placed a new rare antiquity into the room for safe keeping. I was searched in the presence of the Shah. My men took their jobs very seriously."

"They were *your* men, now weren't they? That leads me to believe that you had them ignore the fact that you had taken it and let you walk out with it."

Hessam's anger began to boil like water in a tea kettle and his words spewed like the steam from its spout. "The Shah was standing next to me the entire time we were in the treasury room. Is it he that makes these accusations or is it you?"

"It is I who accuses you but I know that once I have retrieved the Red Diamond of Nadirijna from you then the Shah will certainly call for your execution."

"How is it that it has taken you almost twenty-two years to realize that the gem is missing? Isn't that going to be hard to explain to the Shah? I'm assuming you haven't told him that his rare gem is missing or you wouldn't be alive."

"Whether the Shah knows or not is irrelevant. There are only two people that could've taken it and would've benefitted from doing so; you are one of them and the other would've been that vile assassin, Erik. Being that he has been dead for years makes it all the more logical that you would've been the one to have taken it."

"Yes, and as you can see for yourself, I have benefitted so much from owning such a rare gem. Look around you, sir. I live in a two room flat that hardly accommodates the few possessions I've been able to acquire with the few hundred francs that the Persian treasury still sends me. And if I had stolen the gem don't you think that I would have stopped taking the money from the treasury by now and moved somewhere in which no one could find me?" He licked his busted lip, trying to keep the blood from dripping down his chin. "Your theory is flawed and has more holes in it than a honeycomb. You sir, will need to do better than that to prove that I or even Erik took the Red Diamond of Nadirijna."

The man with the scar put his face close to Hessam's, looking into his bloodied eyes. He rose and then slapped him across the face. "You insult my intelligence. I know that you and Erik were friends and that it was you who helped him escape. So, with that bit of information it is only right to assume that the two of you were in it together."

"I'm telling you sir I know nothing of this rare gem or its whereabouts. It's strange to me that there has been almost twenty-two years of opportunity for someone to have taken this gem and yet you are focused only on the time that I was employed there along with Erik. There is something you haven't divulged; something that has helped you to narrow the time frame in which this gem went missing. What is it?"

"That would suit you to know just how I've deduced that it was you or your disgusting friend who had taken the gem but I won't divulge such crucial information to you. You are likely to use it to create a reason as to why it could not have happened."

"I don't need your information to create a reason as to why it couldn't have happened. I know it as fact that I didn't take the gem from its resting place in the treasury room. It would've been an impossible feat for anyone. The room was guarded by not one or two men but four and everyone who entered and exited was searched thoroughly. Even the Shah would have to sign out what he took from the room. I can tell you with certainty that I wasn't the one who took the precious Red Diamond of Nadirijna."

"And I guess I'm supposed to take your word for it. Is that what you're saying?"

"Yes, and you have my permission to search my flat if you like. I have nothing to hide from you. Your questioning is futile and it is beginning to bore me. So, if we are done here, I would appreciate it if you would untie me and let me clean my wounds."

"You truly believe that I'm going to release you after you have provided me nothing at all to help me in my recovery of the gem."

"Unless you decide to divulge your crucial information I can't begin to help you unravel your mystery and it does seem that you do need my help. And, I can only assume that if you kill me then you'll never get the answers to your questions. So, either way, I'm the one who holds the key to unlocking the doors that may lead you to your final destination."

"You seem quite confident that I won't be able to prove that you had anything to do with this crime, so I'll oblige you and tell you what I know. And I assure you that after you've been told, you'll see why you have been made an accomplice to this crime."

Hessam continued to listen as he tried to keep from showing that he was in extreme pain from his wounds. It was always wise to make the assailant unaware that he had actually caused any discomfort at all. He had been taught that this would serve as bargaining power and would make his assailant aware that he was not dealing with a weak person.

The man with the scar took a seat on the top of the coffee table that Hessam's chair had been placed next to and began his story about the Red Diamond of Nadirijna. "The items in the treasury room are being moved to a newer, more secure building. It was during the removal and appraisal of the items that the diamond was found to be missing. The box in which it had been kept was locked but upon opening it, the appraisers viewed the diamond and with further scrutiny identified it not as a red diamond but a ruby that had been cut to look like the red diamond it was replacing. It was a very clever idea obviously, since it had fooled the Shah for more than twenty-two years. The fact that he never had a need or a desire to open the box of the cursed jewel also helped in its going unnoticed for a long period of time."

"So, how does this secure my alleged participation in its disappearance? Isn't it possible that someone just misplaced it inside the treasury room?"

"We had hoped that this was the case but after accounting for all of the items, the Red Diamond of Nadirijna was nowhere to be found. However, after the room had been emptied and the jewels relocated to their new location, the Shah ordered that the room be renovated and made into a private study where he could put his own personal belongings and spoils on display. During this renovation the builders discovered a trap door that had been built into the floor of the treasury room which opened up into a passageway that tunneled almost the entire length of the palace and exited beyond the walls. A passageway and trap door in which the Shah had no knowledge and he knew of only one person who would be able to contrive such a device to hide his deceit. That person was none other than your friend Erik."

Hessam was astonished at the story he had just been told. He knew nothing of this trap door or the tunnel that led to a place outside the walls of the palace. Erik had never once confided in him about this and at this moment he was very glad that he hadn't.

"You're right sir. Erik is the only person I know that would've been able to build such a device and in all likelihood it probably was he who did build it. However, I had no knowledge of such a trap door or I would've ordered it closed up and would've reported it to the Shah. I may not have believed that the Shah was right in putting Erik and the others to death but I certainly wouldn't want the treasures of Persia stolen. Many a great warrior had lost their lives in order for those gems and antiquities to be gained. I would have killed him myself h~ ˙ known about such treachery."

"I'm inclined to believe you. Your face has told me all that I needed to know. You didn't know about the trap door it is obvious. However, you do know more about Erik than most people and perhaps you may know what he would've done with it."

He knew exactly what he had done with it but he wasn't about to tell this man anything. No, he would produce a story with sound substance to it that would satisfy this torturing menace's appetite for what he would take as the truth about what his friend would have done with such a gem.

"Knowing Erik hardly makes me an expert on what he would've done with the diamond if he did in fact steal it. Since his life was cut short even after I saved him from his execution it would only be speculation as to what he would or could have done with it in such a short time. He probably hid it somewhere near the shores of the sea in which he washed up. There is no telling where he hid it. I don't recall them finding it on his body when they retrieved it from the shore so it is either in the sea or Erik, in his death conjured the best magic trick of all….the disappearing red diamond."

"You're making light of a very serious situation Daroga. It is my head that will be gone if I don't find that cursed red diamond. I would think that the Shah would have been glad that someone had relieved him of its presence but it seems that the importance of the lesson that was taught by the Red Diamond of Nadirijna outweighs the possible curse that it may put upon the person that possesses it."

The Persian knew of the lesson that the man spoke of all too well. It was many years ago during the eighteenth century that the Shah Nadirijna ruled. He had two sons and the eldest had plotted to kill him in order to seize the position of Shah. The son had stolen the red diamond from the treasury room and used it to pay the man that was to assassinate his father. The Shah learned of his plot to kill him and disrupted them by having the assassin killed and the red diamond brought back to him along with his son. He had hoped that his son would apologize for such an act against him but instead his son was obstinate and refused to admit any wrong doing. The Shah then ordered that his son's right hand be cut off and his left eye be put out. From that day forward the gem was known as the Red Diamond of Nadirijna and he kept it in a box near his bed to remind him that even family could not be trusted inside the ranks of his palace. After the Shah Nadirijna was murdered by his other son, the red diamond was put into the treasury room with the rest of the plunder that had been acquired. Through the years, any Shah that had taken the gem out of the treasury room, soon thereafter, suffered a fate not unlike that of Shah Nadirijna. That is why it was always locked inside its box and was never looked at by any Shah after the eighteenth century had passed.

The Persian knew that this man wouldn't stop until he was certain he had followed every lead and every path that could possibly show him where the rare gem had been hidden. So, he decided to send him on the wildest of goose chases he could fabricate.

"Erik once told me that he had traveled all over the world but his most favorite place was India. He had told me that if he ever quit living as he did that is where he would return and make a life for himself. After I set him free, he had at least a day or two to either hide the gem or to send it ahead to a place in India where he hoped to live out his days. It's likely that the diamond is sitting in a postal office somewhere waiting to be claimed."

"Daroga, you have been most helpful in your deductions of the whereabouts of the stolen property of the Shah. It's a shame that he couldn't have kept you in his services. It is also a shame that I have to do what I am about to do now."

The man with the scar under his eye pulled out a dagger and then pressed the tip of it into his cheek, cutting a small wound in it.

"I know that Erik is not dead and I have known that he wasn't dead for many years now but never had any reason to come looking for him until now. Yes, the friends you left behind that helped dress the corpse in Erik's clothes had their price for telling me what really happened to the deformed monster that you thought was worth saving all those years ago. I also know that the Opera Ghost that lived underneath the Paris Opera House had a description that matched that of Erik's. His disgusting face of death and his carnival magic being used to torment and terrorize the people of the Opera House, it was all too easy to figure out that he was still alive. However, it would seem that he met his death naturally and you sir are the one that identified his body. How is it that you could identify a man that had no flesh on his bones? You must have supernatural powers that the rest of us don't possess."

The Persian was now very frightened because of what had just been revealed to him. He knew now he would probably not live to see the next hour. He knew that he would have to think quickly if we wanted to save his own neck along with Erik's. These men surely wouldn't give up until he gave them something that sounded like the truth.

"It was easy for me to identify his remains for I had visited him in the catacombs of the Opera House at least a dozen times. He showed me where he had planned his resting place to be since near death, dying of whatever illness a man in his condition wo been plagued with since he had been born with a face of dea me that he would be wearing a gold ring on his finger so that if I was unable to come to him in a sufficient amount of time, I would know that it was truly his body."

The assailant didn't believe the story but played along just to see what information he would be able to give him. "You expect me to believe this story after you already lied to me about this gypsy's corpse being found on the shore of the sea? I think you must think that I am easily fooled."

"No sir, I do not. I think that you know the truth and that you are just refusing to believe it because it would mean the end to your search. A dead man can't show you where he put a jewel."

"You're right, he can't but you can. He must have told you something about this rare gem or at least given you some hint that he had something of value in his possession."

"I don't recall him ever talking about anything other than the music he loved to play. However, if he had any treasures I can almost say with certainty that he would have kept them in the fifth cellar of the Opera House which is where he resided."

"Then I assume that you will be able to take me there and help in the search."

"I'm not so sure that I can. You see, Erik never allowed anyone entry into his home. I was only allowed to meet him in the passageways and landings. I can get you to the entrance of the lower cellar but as far as knowing how to enter or even find his well hidden lair that will be entirely up to you. You know as well as I do that if Erik didn't want you to find one of his hidden doors it was almost guaranteed that you wouldn't."

"Then it is settled, you will guide me to the entrance of the lower cellar and I shall try my luck at finding this house in which he lived. And if you don't agree to do so then it is only fitting that I take your life."

Hessam nodded his head in agreement and did his best not to let the fear show in his face or be heard in his voice. He couldn't help but wonder what had happened to Darius and why he hadn't intervened on his behalf. He knew that courageous acts were not something that Darius excelled in but he thought that perhaps he might at least have tried to cause a distraction of some kind to ward his assailants off. Nevertheless, it was decided that he would show these two men to the entrance of the lower cellar in hopes that they may possibly spare his life for at least a few more hours.

Courageous

They cleaned the daroga up, gave him some fresh clothes to change into and then escorted him down to the cab. After a few minutes Darius, who was not sure of what had just transpired but knew it was not favorable, opened the window, climbed back into the room where he had been before the visitors had come and sat on the edge of the small bed in which he slept. He knew that he should go help the daroga but he wasn't quite sure how. He suspected that anything he would tell the officials would only create more problems and raise more questions about things in which they didn't need to know. Staying at the flat was no longer safe and so he decided to go to the flat of Amalie's uncle that used to reside in Paris. Amalie had offered it to them many times as suitable living quarters since it was much bigger than where they were living but Hessam wouldn't accept it. He was a man that took great pride in providing for himself and his devoted servant. However, this was the perfect opportunity to find out just how wonderful her uncle's flat was. He packed a couple of bags with his and Hessam's belongings, found the key in which Amalie had given to them and left the small flat.

When the cab came to the Rue Scribe the two men and the Persian got out and began walking toward the opening in which the Persian had spoken. There was water in the canal but as they neared the entrance they could see the rat catcher's walkway that hugged the walls of the canal which stood centimeters above the water, allowing enough room for someone to pass.

"This is the entrance? You'd better not be lying to me Daroga."

"Yes, that is the entrance. This is how I always entered when Erik wished to speak to me. Lower yourself down to the walkway and then follow it until you reach the open lake. You'll find an arch that is gated but the gate is not mired down. There is a lever at the bottom of the lake that will make it rise. This will give you entrance into the first and only chamber of Erik's house in which I was ever permitted to meet him."

"This lever you speak of, it is at the bottom of the lake?"

"Yes, and you will have to dive into the water to pull it in order to release the gate."

"Daroga, you surely didn't have to dive into the lake every time you met with Erik. There has to be another way."

"You're right, I didn't have to dive into the lake because the lake was not at the level it is now. They have since flooded parts of the lower catacombs to relieve the pressure that the waters have created on the foundation of the Opera House. When I was last here the lever was above water and was disguised to look like a holder for a torch. As for there being another way, I don't know of any. This is the only way I ever entered the cellars. If you don't wish to dive into the water, you may wait for six months after they have pumped the majority of it out and then return to find what you seek."

"I don't have time to wait, so I guess you will enjoy the swim that you are about to take Daroga."

"I'm afraid that's impossible. I never learned to swim and if you were to throw me into the water I would drown and then your lever would still not be pulled."

The assailant with the scar was growing impatient and was tiring of the delays. He took the daroga by the arm, holding his revolver to his chin.

"Well, then I guess you will pull it quickly and get back to the top of the water so that I may rescue you."

Then he took the daroga and pushed him into the water. Hessam flailed in a panic, screaming for help and then began to sink quickly. What his assailants didn't realize was that he was not only a good liar but a very good swimmer. He made it look as if he were drowning and then quickly made his way in the murky water to the lever, he pulled it and the gate began to open but then he pulled it again, stopping it in mid-rise. He removed his waistcoat under the water so that he would be able to swim better and hoped it would float to the top so that his captors would think he was dead. He then swam underneath the gate to where he knew was a drainage tunnel. The path of the tunnel flowed underneath the walls of the hidden home. It led to the trap door that was in the torture chamber. The daroga remembered all too well how he and Raoul had narrowly escaped drowning when Christine had chosen to turn the grasshopper which in turn triggered the sinking of the gun powder which rose the level of the water causing the torture chamber to become flooded, almost drowning he and Raoul. However, now this trap door would not be for villainy but for salvation. He pushed his way through the flow of draining water and grabbed the narrow metal ladder that was hung from the trap door that would soon lead to his freedom. He pushed up on the slightly opened door above him, heard it drop to one side of the floor and quickly climbed up the ladder and entered the torture chamber. After pushing open the door that was slightly ajar that led out of the torture chamber, he glanced at the quiet lake house and all that had been left behind. He took a moment to catch his breath and then waited patiently. He thought about the time he had spent with Erik in his residence. How he had once thought that his madness would consume him and eventually cause his death. It seemed to be a lifetime ago that he had tried to persuade him from continuing his delusional relationship with Christine. He was glad that Erik had finally realized that love wasn't something one could capture; it was something that was created. He had found that with Amalie and for that Hessam was very thankful. It occurred to him that Erik's life had been much like his home. It didn't allow anyone in, unless they knew the secrets of how to open it up. It was unfortunate that the one time he had allowed someone in, they nearly destroyed it too. But like the bulkhead walls in which his home had been built inside, he was strong and no matter what the world would throw at him he would weather it. Now, his home had become a refuge for not taking a life but saving one. The gate that he had led the two men to would let them in, but if they didn't know where the door that lay inside the gate above the water was hidden, they wouldn't have any chance of ever reaching the interior of the lake house. Which in reality didn't matter anyway because what they sought was not there. No, it was somewhere that they would never think to look.

The two men stood on the walkway waiting for the gate to complete its rise into the air but it never did. Within a few minutes, the scar faced man turned to his colleague and pushed him into the water.

"Find him, or pull the lever, I don't care which just make sure you do one or the other or you will not be coming back with me."

Just about the time the man was about to dive under the water, he saw the daroga's waistcoat make its way to the top of the water. He swam to it and pulled it out, handing it to his superior.

"I guess he really wasn't a very good swimmer. It's just as well; his time with us was borrowed only for my own reasons. Now find that lever so that we may find our treasure."

His colleague dove into the water, scaling the wall among the reeds and moss trying to find the lever. He hoped that he wouldn't come face to face with the drowned Persian but knew that he would be rewarded well if he could retrieve the body. Even with his eyes wide open it was nearly impossible to see directly in front of him. The filth from the water was stinging his eyes but he finely felt his way to a long object that felt like the torch holder that the Persian had described. He tugged on it and nothing happened. He tugged again and the gate began to open slowly. As the gate opened the man came up out of the water, gasping for air. He swam to the ledge and his superior helped him out.

"I couldn't see the daroga's body anywhere, but the water is so dark that I was glad to find the lever."

"It is fine my friend, we don't need his body. When they do find it, they will think it was an accident. Now let's go get what we came to find."

The two men jumped over the empty space that divided the rat catcher's walkway to allow the gate to block the path when closed. They walked to the stairs that wound around the bulkhead. They looked for any possible way to enter as they walked slowly and carefully around the rat catcher's walkway that passed around the bulkhead walls. There was no sign that anyone ever had lived where Hessam had told them Erik was to have lived.

"There's nothing here," said the scar faced man. "I think Hessam has lied to us."

"Maybe the house is underneath the water. He did say that they had flooded the lower level and were in the process of pumping the water out. Perhaps, we will have to return at a later date, in order to retrieve what we came to get."

The scar faced man rubbed his chin and then scratched his head. "Yes, that would make perfect sense but then why would the daroga bring us down here if he knew he wouldn't be able to show us the lake house?"

"Danush, maybe he just wanted to save his own life. I think I would have done the same."

"I suppose that could be the reason Fardin, but maybe he had another reason for bringing us here. It's possible that he knew the Red Diamond of Nadirijna was not here to begin with and was keeping us from where it was really hidden."

"And where would that be sir?"

"His flat, Fardin, his flat is where it is! Now that he is dead we may have as much time as we like to find it. Come, let's make our way back to the hotel, get you a change of clothes and go back to his flat."

The two men left the Opera House cellars the same way they entered. The Persian, who had been sitting quietly in the lake house near the hidden door that led to the stairs that wound around the bulkhead, waited for the men to leave and then waited another thirty minutes or so to be sure that they had left. He could have left through the trick door that exited into the third floor cellar but had decided to stay in order to hear their plans. He knew that once they couldn't get in, they wouldn't give up quickly and besides, he couldn't risk the gate being left open. He entered the water through the man hole, closing it behind him, swam to the lever and pushed it upward, causing it to lower back into the water. He then pulled himself out onto the walkway and rested for a moment. He picked up his waistcoat, which the two men had left behind and laid it across his arm. It was a very nice waistcoat and it was one of his favorites, he couldn't bear to leave it behind. He then made his exit out of the cellars and onto the Rue Scribe.

It was there that he was greeted by a whistle and a wave of a hand through an open door of a cab. He recognized the face that soon replaced the arm that had been waving furiously at him. It was Darius. After he had gone to the flat of Amalie's uncle, he made his way to the Rue Scribe and waited. Once he saw the two men leave, he was hesitant to enter into the cellars just in case they were to come back. So he waited. It was when he was about to embark from the cab that he noticed his friend, walking up the street. The Persian, who was still very wet, entered the cab and took a seat next to Darius.

"What happened to you? Did they try to drown you?"

"No, Darius, I voluntarily drowned myself. I'll explain everything in detail later. The two men are bent to return to our flat to search it for the red diamond."

"Don't worry sir, they won't find it there," Darius reassured him.

"I know that Darius but I'm worried that they will find the correspondence that I have kept with Erik as of late."

"They won't sir."

"How can you be so certain?"

"Because I took the liberty of doing as you have always prepared me to do. I packed the small box of your most private belongings along with some of your clothing and fled from the flat as quickly as possible."

"And just where did you go Darius?"

"I took the key that Madame Geraurd gave to you for her uncle's flat and I took our bags there. I hope that what I have done has pleased you."

The Persian leaned toward Darius and said, "You may not be the most courageous man I know but your ability to follow instructions is most amiable. I couldn't have executed a better plan myself."

"I'm glad that you think so sir."

The cab continued to drive down the streets of Paris as the Persian and Darius planned what they would do next. Even though they had a safe place on the other side of town from their old flat, it wasn't wise to stay put for too long. The Persian knew that these two men wouldn't give up until they found what they intended him to provide them. They would be back at the Opera House in six months, he was certain of it. He knew that when they were unsuccessful at finding the Red Diamond of Nadirijna in his flat they would have no other choice but to believe his story that Erik had probably hidden it within the cellars of the Opera House.

Did You See It

The years had passed so quickly and Louisa was now six years old. She had the beauty and intelligence of her mother and the charisma and charm of her father. Her wavy brown hair bounced as she moved across the drawing room floor where she greeted her father, Erik, while he played the piano.

"Good morning, Father. Isn't it time for my lesson?"

"Yes, Louisa it is. However, I've decided that today we will put your piano lessons away for a later time and we'll work more on your magic."

"Oh, Father, can we?"

"Yes, and I'm going to teach you something new today because you have already mastered everything else I have taught you thus far."

"Are you going to finally teach me how to use the powder Father?"

"I'm not sure that you're ready for the powder, Louisa. It takes concentration, steady hands and precise execution to master the powder."

"But Father I will never master something that I'm not given the time to practice."

"Louisa, for a six year old you're quite the negotiator. All right, I'll show you how to use the powder, but remember that you may only practice using it outside on the terrace when I'm with you. Do you understand Louisa?'

"Yes, Father, I understand."

Erik took his daughter's small hand as they walked out of the drawing room and from the back entrance of the house they made their way out onto the terrace. He led her to a bench and on the edge sat a package. Louisa sat down on the bench and picked it up. She examined it and then handed it to Erik. He politely refused to take it from her and said, "Go ahead Louisa, open it. It's for you."

"It's for me. It's not even my birthday." She ripped the paper off of the package and pulled out a large black piece of fabric. She didn't know what to make of it at first but upon further examination she saw that it was a cloak with a black hood.

"It's just like Mother's. Thank you Father."

"You're welcome. It may look like your mother's but it's quite different if you take a closer look at it."

"What do you mean Father?"

"Give it to me Louisa and I'll show you."

She handed it to her father and he fastened it around her. He took one side of the cloak, holding the inside of it up where she could see it.

"Look here." He pointed to a slit that had been cut into the fabric. "This is a hidden pocket and the other side of your cloak has another one just like this one. Put your hand in it."

Louisa did as she was told. She reached slowly into the slit and her fingers made their descent into the pocket that was just big enough for her small hand. When it reached the bottom she felt something smooth and soft. She pulled it out and smiled as she looked at her father.

"It's the pouch of powder isn't it Father?"

"Yes, my child, it is."

"I think I know where the flint and metal piece is Father." She fumbled around the other side of her cloak and found the pocket. She slipped her hand into it and retrieved the two items she would also need in order to master the art of using the magical dust.

"I found them, Father." She marveled at the items that she had pulled from her cloak and then smiled at Erik.

"Thank you Father. This is going to be the best day we have ever had together." She threw her arms around her Father's waist and hugged him tightly. He put his hand on the top of her; stroking it lightly.

"Yes, my dear child, this will be one of many wonderful days that we'll spend together. Now if you're ready, I'll teach you the first thing you need to know in order to be able to use the powder."

They stayed out on the terrace practicing how to get the flint to light with just one stroke of it across the piece of metal that Erik had designed to work together to create a quick spark that would ignite the magic dust causing a large flash and enough smoke to allow the magician using it time to disappear. The flint was shaped like a thimble that could be worn on the middle finger and the metal that was to be used to strike it against was an actual thimble that was to be placed on the thumb. When the fingers were snapped it would create a quick spark that would light the string on the bag that was a fuse. This would allow the magician enough time to throw the magic powder bag down and allow for his escape. Louisa tried for an hour until her fingers became sore and tired. She wasn't any closer to mastering this task than before she started. She was growing frustrated but she was determined not to let her previous failures keep her from having at least one success. As she made many more attempts to get a spark to appear they were interrupted by Amalie's concerned voice, "Erik, what is it that you're trying to teach our child? Don't you think that playing with your magic powder is a bit dangerous for her?"

Erik rose to his feet while signaling Louisa to continue to practice. He walked over to Amalie, kissed her on the cheek and smiled. "My love, she is in no danger. I'm keeping a close eye on her and although she is young she is quite capable of mastering this skill. It will take more than one lesson for her to be able to get the flint to create a spark." Just as he finished his sentence a thunderous boom and a pillar of smoke came from behind them along with the cheers of a small voice. "I did it Father, I did it!" Erik turned to her and said, "Why, yes you did and quite well, I might add." Amalie gave him a disapproving look and ran to her daughter, hugged her and checked her for burns or any other injury that she may have received from the small explosion.

"Are you alright Louisa?"

"Yes, Mother I'm fine. Did you see how I made the smoke? Did you see?" Louisa's smile erased the anger that had been on her mother's face.

"Yes, my love, I saw it and it was quite magnificent. You understand that you're only to practice this trick with your Father attending you? Tell me that you understand this Louisa."

"Of course, Mother. It wouldn't be any fun if Father wasn't here to see me do it."

"Good, I'm relieved to hear that you're in agreement with me. Now go put your new cloak away in your room and wash your hands. I baked some cookies and you may have two of them."

The small child skipped happily into the house leaving Erik and Amalie alone. He walked up behind her putting his arms around her and clasping his hands in front of her waist like a chain binding her to him. He kissed her once more on the cheek and spoke softly in her ear. "I love you."

"I love you, too. However, that doesn't excuse you from putting our child's life in danger."

"She's perfectly fine Amalie. She's a brave little girl. She reminds me of someone else who lives in this house."

"And who might that be?" she said with sarcasm in her voice.

"Oh, a certain woman that was brave enough to love a man like me."

"You may think that it was brave for me to love you but in my heart I knew it was the only choice I would have to make in order to be happy for the rest of my life." She turned around, still bound in his human chain and kissed him. "However, if this is your attempt to change the subject it has failed. I truly wish you wouldn't teach her the more complicated and dangerous tricks from your days of creating magic. I didn't mind the sleight of hand tricks and even the illusions of legerdemain were fine but the magic powder could truly cause her harm."

"I know that you're concerned but Amalie, she is an only child and the magic doesn't only entertain her but it helps to broaden her senses, her mind. I will only give her lessons on how to use the powder twice a week and you may join us for the lesson if you wish. Will that satisfy your concern?"

"I assume that if I said no, you would continue to teach her anyway so I believe my only recourse is to agree to your terms." She gave him the disapproving look once more but it was followed by a crooked smile that let him know that she was pacified by his compromise.

"Very well then, it's settled. Now I'd like to have a few of those cookies you spoke of earlier."

"They're in the kitchen and could you please make sure that Louisa has washed before she gets them from the cookie jar?"

He kissed her on the cheek and said, "I will," as he left her standing alone on the terrace in the warm sun. She walked to the potted plants which she and Louisa had planted, pushed her finger into the soil and determined that they could wait another day before they would need watering. The sun was warm upon her face and it seemed to invite her to linger in its glow, relaxing her, helping her to think of a way to break the news to him that she was needed in Etrepagny by someone unfortunate and very ill who required her medical skills. The sun lured her into its arms of sunbeams, caressing her shoulders as she sat on the small bench on the edge of the terrace. She would be content if allowed to stay in the scenic beauty of the landscape that was before her. Taking a trip to Etrepagny would certainly not be something she wanted to do without Erik but she didn't believe he would dare to go with her. His safety and happiness rested at the chateau where he would spend countless hours with his daughter teaching her his cunning tricks of illusion and helping her to understand the finer points of music and ventriloquism. She was only six but she had a mind that soaked up his knowledge just as a towel soaked up water spilled from a cup. He lavished her with his attention so much that Amalie dared not interfere for fear that he would withdraw his affections from her. However, in his quest for showing his love for her she was never to be considered spoiled. She knew right from wrong due to the hour long Bible readings Erik had made a routine with her before she could even mutter the words "Father". He felt that this was one way that he could repay the kindness of his old friend, Louisa's grandfather, and while doing so he also learned a great deal about his own belief in God. Of course, etiquette and manners were something that her father taught her first although he always made sure that she knew that she was to think for herself and not just do what everyone else was doing merely to satisfy societal rules. Discipline was fair and just at his hands but it was never cruel and destructive. He had learned from his own experiences that sometimes pain was something better left for others to inflict on his child because eventually they would and there would not be anything he could do to stop it. He could only be there to manage the pain and the recovery. Perhaps if she took Louisa with her to Etrepagny it would ease her mind about taking the trip. It wasn't that she didn't trust him with her; she was worried that in her absence he would continue to conduct the magic powder trick and she would come home to a burned child.

She rose from the bench and began her walk to the back entrance when she heard her name being yelled from a distance. She spun on her heels quickly to see who had called for her. She saw no one but heard the voice again. Erik came through the back door and saw the bewildered look upon her face.

"What's wrong Amalie? Your face is as white as a sheet."

"Did you hear it? Did you hear the voice calling my name?"

"Yes and I'm afraid that you've been the victim of Louisa's fine talent."

Just then Louisa appeared from the corner of the house that was the furthest from her parents. She was laughing wildly at her mother. Erik walked to her and took her by the hand.

"Louisa, I want you to apologize to your mother. You frightened her and I have told you before that your talent is not to be used to play tricks on your elders or anyone else for that matter. Now tell your mother you're sorry and then you will go straight to your room and not come out until supper."

"But Father, I was only practicing like you told me too."

"Louisa, I told you to practice in your room, not where others could hear you. Now do as I have told you."

Louisa began to cry. "But......but....Father!"

Erik's face turned from disappointment to anger at his child's will-fulness. She knew by his turn in moods that she should not press the issue. She turned to her mother and apologized and then with a sullen look upon her face went to her room.

"I'm sorry my love. I'll give her a stern talking to before supper."

"She's only six Erik; she was bound to try it at least once. I'm sure she has learned her lesson. She is quite good at throwing her voice."

"I could teach you if you like," he smiled as he took her hand in his and they began walking to the back entrance.

"No thank you. I am content to heal the sick which incidentally is what I had originally come out onto the terrace to speak with you about earlier."

They entered the house, walked through the kitchen, down the hall, passed through the foyer, entered the great room and took a seat upon the sofa that sat in front of the fireplace.

"Reverend Troudeaux has asked me to visit a young widow who has a young daughter that aspires to become a doctor. The widow is ill and they don't have funds for a doctor to pay her a visit. The Reverend has offered to pay for my room and board as well as the fee that I would charge."

"You're not honestly going to accept the Reverend's money, are you Amalie?"

She rolled her eyes at him and said, "Of course not. You and Peter have done very well with your business endeavor with you as the architect and he as the business contact and manager of the finances. I should say that you will build most of the chateaus across France. You have provided for us very well." She took his hand and then kissed it. "No, it's not about the money. However, I would like to go tend to this woman and help her daughter."

"Well, then go. You're one of the finest doctor's around. I know that you haven't been able to acquire a practice of your own but your reputation in the village has begun to spread among the neighboring villages. I believe that most of the women prefer you to Dr. Reneau."

"Yes, I agree with your observations that the women prefer me and for that I am thankful. My soaring popularity has kept me abreast of my medical procedures but my reputation isn't what compels me to want to see this woman and it is not what has given me reservations about asking your permission to go see her." She began to fidget with her skirt. She stood up and began pacing back and forth like a soldier guarding the entrance to a palace.

"The woman lives in Etrepagny. I would have to be gone for at least four or five days, maybe more."

"I see. That is quite a long time to be away from Louisa and from me. Why or what is it that compels you to go help this woman? What do you know about her?"

Amalie sat back down, looking straight into his cool blue eyes. She sat quietly for a moment searching them to see if his eyes would tell her if his questions were meant to give reason to deny her or if they were meant merely to satisfy his own curiosity. She couldn't see a glimmer of either in them. Instead she saw the loving eyes that would give her anything if she asked.

"It was something the Reverend said to me about the manner in which her husband died."

"And what was that?" He leaned forward eager to hear what the Reverend had told her.

"He said that he had met his death at the hands of a man who murdered his three year old son."

His eyes became wider, his face pale with grief for the life of a man and a child he didn't know. The thought of someone hurting his own child flashed through his mind and stabbed at his heart, not knowing that he could ever have been affected by only the thought of something so cruel and unnecessary.

"Did he say why this young boy and his father were murdered?"

"No, only that since the day it happened the widow left the village in which they had been living and settled in Etrepagny where no one would ever know of their hardship."

"Then how is it that the Reverend knows them?"

"The man was his cousin's son. She is part of his family therefore I feel that I must go, especially after everything he has done for us."

He knew she was right. The Reverend Troudeaux had been very instrumental in their acceptance into the village and especially the church congregation after Frederic's death. He made sure that everyone knew that it wasn't Erik who had killed him but that he was a man protecting his family and a man in need of a family beyond the one that he had on earth. He had Erik fill in as the pianist on every fourth Sunday so that Madame Blanc could sit with her husband during the services. It was after he had begun playing in Madame Blanc's absence that he won over the villagers of Trie-Chateau. No one had ever heard a hymn brought to life without the voices that were meant to accompany the music until they had heard Erik put his fingers upon the black and white keys of the piano that sat in the corner of the church. The hymns would rise into the air and although no voices were lifted in song it was as if they were audible in every individual's ears that bore witness to the music. His music worshipped God's omnipotent powers and cleansed the souls of all who heard it.

It was then that Madame and Monsieur Blanc not only welcomed him into the house in which they worshipped but she gave him her position as pianist and it was she who would play on every fourth Sunday. Monsieur Blanc had concluded and even verbally confessed to the Reverend and Erik that his gift of music was certainly from God. Although he thought he was the most unlikely of persons to be used to give this wonderful gift to the world, no one could deny or doubt that the gift they had all received through his fingers upon the keys was something that should be used to worship their Lord. Therefore, he was privileged and humbled to have him worship alongside him.

Yes, he owed the Reverend Troudeaux a lot more than most people and if sending his wife to help a dear family member of his was the payment for his generosity and friendship then it would certainly not be at his hands that his wife's skills would be withheld.

"Amalie, if you must go then I will go with you and so will Louisa. We'll make it into a family holiday."

"Are you certain that you will be comfortable leaving the chateau? Are you sure that Peter can do without you?"

"I don't see why not. I'm always comfortable as long as I'm with you and I have already given to Peter that which he requires for the next building project. I'm sure he can spare my charm and wit for the next four or five days," he laughed as he took her hand and then pulled her closely to him so that he could gaze into her eyes. "Peter is quite capable of faking his knowledge about erecting buildings until I return. It will only be for a few days. He couldn't possibly cause too much trouble until I return."

Amalie kissed him gently on his lips, gave him a quick embrace and then freed herself from his grasp. "I guess I better start packing our things for the trip. The Reverend has arranged for our departure the day after tomorrow."

"Oh he did, did he? He arranged for *all of us* to be traveling?" he said with sarcasm in his voice.

"Why yes, he wasn't sure you would go with me but he knew you would send someone to escort your daughter and I. He knows how protective you are of your family." She gave a smile and a slight nod to him as she walked up the staircase.

"The Reverend seems to know more about me than I thought he did," he laughed. "I'll go tell Louisa about our upcoming trip and send her to help you with the packing."

"Thank you, and be sure to pay a visit to Peter to let him know that you'll be leaving and I'll let Meg and Chester know so that they may watch the house for us." She finished her ascension up the staircase and disappeared into their bedroom. Erik walked up the stairs and down the hall to Louisa's room. There he found her standing on her bed playing with her cloak; wrapping and unwrapping her small body in and out of it. When she saw him enter the room she shrank into a small ball on top of her bed; her legs pulled to her chest and her arms clinging tightly around her knees.

"Yes, Father, I know I'm not supposed to stand on my bed. I'm sorry, it won't happen again," she said with a very saddened tone in her voice.

"Well at least not until we return from Etrepagny anyway," he smiled at her as her head rose from where it had been resting on top of her knees.

"Etrepagny, why are we going there?"

He sat on the edge of the bed and put his hand on her knees. "Your mother has been asked to help a sick widow woman there and you and I are going to go to keep her company."

"Do you think there are other children there that I can play with Father?"

"Oh, I'm not sure Louisa. I know this woman has a young daughter but I'm not sure how old she is or if she has other children. I guess we'll just have to wait and see when we get there."

"My first real adventure Father and we all get to take it together." She sat up on her knees and threw her arms around her Father's neck and kissed his disfigured cheek.

"Does this mean I'm not in trouble anymore?"

"Have you learned your lesson Louisa?"

"Yes, Father. I know that scaring Mother wasn't very nice. I promise I won't ever do it again."

He could tell that she was sincere. He kissed her on the forehead and then grabbed both of her hands. "Very well, then you get the privilege of helping your mother pack for the trip. She's waiting for you in our bedroom. Do everything she asks of you and do it cheerfully."

"Yes, Father, I will." She hugged him again and then rushed out of the room full of excitement and energy to help her mother.

He walked down the hall and down into the study. He sat behind the desk, found the Bible that was once Gaston's but was now his, and began reading. He knew that if he were going to make this trip with his family that he would have to draw his strength not from inside but from God in order to face the world of men and women who may snicker and whisper at the sight of him. This would be the first trip he had taken to a village other than Trie-Chateau in over six years. He was content to stay in the world that he and Amalie had made together along with their friends but he knew that this day would come and that this would be the true test of what he had learned about himself and what God truly had taught him. He had protected Louisa as long as he could from the cruelness of the world that he knew all too well but knew that if she was to have any compassion for others who weren't like her, she would need to witness its cruelties first hand. He would do his best to try to shield her but sometimes learning has to come with pain. He had found that out through his own journey of learning to love someone.

I Beg Your Pardon

The bags were all packed and were being loaded onto the coach as Erik placed his mask over the disfigured portion of his face and attached his hairpiece. As he stood in front of the mirror in his room making sure that it was placed properly where no one could see any part of his birthmark, Louisa came bouncing into the room and stopped abruptly, surprised at what she saw.

"Father, why are you wearing your mask and hairpiece today? You usually only wear them on Sunday's when we go to church."

"Well, it's a special day today. It's our first long trip together as a family and I thought it would be nice to dress up."

"Father, I may only be six but I know that it's because you don't want strangers to see your face," she said with a crooked smile.

"Why do you think I don't want strangers to see my face, Louisa?" he asked her with a genuine longing to hear her answer.

"It's because your face isn't like everyone else's Father. My face doesn't look anything like yours, except for my eyes. How come God didn't give me a face as special as yours Father? I wish I could wear a mask too," she said with sadness in her voice.

Erik was taken aback at his daughter's response. It was true that she had his eyes but for her to long for a misshapen face like his was almost unfathomable to him. She was a child and didn't realize what horrors this face had brought him and it was the innocence of her comment that made his reply so important.

"Louisa, my child, you do have a special face. It is the one that God gave you and it is the only one like it. It resembles some of mine and some of your mother's but most of it is unique only to you. God gives all of us our own special faces for various reasons for which I cannot explain, but someday you'll know why He gave you the face you have." He picked her up and began carrying her to the door.

"Have you figured out why God gave *you* such a special face Father?"

Erik stopped in the doorway and looked into his daughter's eyes which were searching his eyes for an honest answer.

"Yes, Louisa, I think I have." He smiled at her and kissed her on the cheek. "I think God gave me this face so that your mother would be able to find me."

"She did find you Father, she did."

"Yes, she did and I am so happy that she did. I don't know what I'd do without your mother or you for that matter."

"I do," Louisa smiled and patted her father's cheek.

"You do?" Erik smiled back at her.

"You would cry all day and wish for Mother to find you," she laughed.

As Louisa finished her sentence Amalie met them on the staircase. "Why would your father be crying Louisa?"

"He'd be crying because you hadn't found him yet Mother."

"Yes, dear and I too would be crying if I hadn't found him," she kissed Erik on the cheek and then Louisa. "I love you both very much. Now that that's settled, are the two of you ready to go to Etrepagny?"

"We were on our way to the coach when you intercepted us," he said while he began down the stairs.

"I have to get my doctor's bag off the dresser and I'll meet you in the coach." Amalie went into their room, grabbed her doctor's bag and on the way out she realized that she had forgotten to put on her wedding ring. She rarely took it off but the night before she had been sewing a piece of lace back into place on one of her dresses and removed it so as not to snag the delicate fabric with the prongs of her ring. She opened the drawer to her jewelry box, picked it up and put it on her finger. Before she closed the little drawer she noticed the red diamond that the Persian had given to her when they first met. She picked it up and put it into a small box which fit nicely into her doctor's bag. She thought that this would be the perfect opportunity to get it put into a setting for a necklace or a ring since they would be in a village much bigger than theirs. She closed her bag and then made her way downstairs and walked outside where the coach that the Reverend had arranged to carry them to Etrepagny awaited her. She climbed in taking her place next to Erik and the three of them began their journey.

The ride to Etrepagny took the entire morning and most of the afternoon. They arrived two hours before dusk and settled into their room at one of the local inns where the Reverend Troudeaux had arranged for them to stay. After they unpacked their items from their bags they found a small restaurant in which to dine. After enjoying their meal they went back to the inn and turned in for the night.

The morning brought the sun and with it the warm rays that fell upon Amalie's face as she sat up in bed observing her daughter sleeping peacefully on a pallet they made for her on the floor and her husband who was starting to stir from his slumber next to her. She loved them both very much and was so glad that God had blessed her with them. She put her hand on Erik's face, gently touching it and then slowly ran her fingers through his sparsely untamed hair. He looked like a child sometimes when he was sleeping; devoid of worry or anxiousness of what anyone might say to him the first time they laid eyes on him. This trip was truly going to be a test of his reserve and his ability to be able to put his past behind him. She knew that he wouldn't hurt anyone but did he know that about himself. Did he trust in the things that he had learned about the man he truly was enough to be able to walk away from a stranger's ignorance? They would soon find out.

They rose from their beds, dressed and then found a café in which to dine for breakfast. Louisa was asking question after question about all of the new things that she was seeing. He answered her questions while they ate and Amalie prepared herself for her visit with the widow. Before leaving the Reverend had given her a piece of paper that bore the widow's name which was Madame Claire Brun and her daughter's name was Odette. They lived in a small farmhouse outside of town next to her father-in-law Remy Brun. Remy's wife had died just three weeks prior of an unidentifiable infection to her kidneys. It seemed that things were worsening for their family now that Claire had taken ill. The Reverend said that his cousin Remy couldn't bear it if another one of his family members died and that is why he had called upon him not just for prayer but for any other help he could give to him. Amalie knew that she may be their only hope and that is why she sat at the table reading through a recent medical publication hoping that possibly any information she obtained from it would be helpful in assessing the condition of Madame Brun. Erik and Louisa continued their conversation through breakfast and as they finished eating an older gentleman with a worn but kind face approached the table.

"Monsieur, I'm the owner of this establishment and I'm afraid I'm going to have to ask you to leave at once," he said softly so as not to draw attention.

Amalie's eyes met Erik's and he smiled at her. She knew that smile all too well and it meant that he was about to start something she was afraid he shouldn't.

"May I inquire why we must leave at once sir?" he said politely.

"It isn't I who wishes for you to leave sir but you see…..I have several patrons who are quite frightened that whatever it is you have behind your mask may infect them also," the older man replied nervously.

"I can assure you sir that the only thing under my mask is my intelligence and by their ignorance it is obvious that they have not come close enough for them to become infected with it."

"Monsieur, I don't want any trouble this morning and since you're obviously traveling through, I beg of you to please leave......I wouldn't ask but this café is the only means I have to take care of my family. If I anger my regular patrons they will take their business elsewhere."

Erik's eyes searched the eyes of the owner. He then took a deep breath after a moment of considering his options about how to handle the situation before him.

"I understand sir and I don't wish to cause you any undue harm. It is apparent to me that you're a man in a situation that doesn't serve you either way." He took out his money clip and handed the man twice what he owed him for their breakfast. He then motioned to Amalie and Louisa to rise from the table. The man looked at the money and said, "Monsieur, you've given me too much," as he held out the extra bills for Erik to take back.

"No, Monsieur, you keep it. Your family is very blessed to have a man like you to look after them." He smiled and then took Amalie by the hand and Louisa followed behind them as they walked out onto the sidewalk.

Amalie squeezed his hand tightly and looked up at him as they walked toward the coach that was waiting to take them to Madame Brun's home. "You handled that very well."

"Your words indicate that you're somewhat surprised that I did."

"No, not surprised at all. I believe the word I'm looking for would be proud."

"Well, it wasn't the owner's prejudices that caused him to approach us, just his need to keep his patrons. I admired his discretion and his honesty. There was no reason to be angry with him. Besides, we were finished and when you argue with fools you tend to become one yourself."

She squeezed his hand again and then leaned her head against his shoulder. "Well said Erik, well said."

The Doctor Is In

*A*s the coach pulled into the circular driveway of the small country cottage of Madame Brun, Amalie nervously fumbled through her medical bag taking inventory of the things that she would need first in assessing her new patient's condition.

"Amalie, everything will be fine. There's no need to be nervous. You're a good doctor and anything you'll be able to do for her will be better than what she has now, which is nothing."

"I don't want it to be *just* good enough for her; I want it to be what she needs to get better. The Reverend Troudeaux is counting on me."

"Well, you can't help her unless you get out of the coach," he smiled and then let out a slight chuckle.

"Come on Mother. Let's go have an adventure."

They all exited the coach, walked to the front door and then Erik lightly knocked on the door. They waited patiently for several minutes but no one came. He knocked again but this time much louder. Another minute passed and still no one came to the door. Louisa had made use of her good detective skills and was peering into the house from the front window. She could see a girl sitting in a chair but she wasn't moving.

"Mother, Father, there is a girl in a chair. She is either asleep or dead because she isn't moving."

"Louisa, get away from the window. It isn't polite to peer into windows," her mother scolded.

Erik knocked again but this time he yelled, "Is there anyone home? It's Dr. Geraurd and she has come to help Madame Brun."

Louisa disobeyed her mother and continued to look through the window. This time she noticed something that frightened her and made her cry. "Mother, there's blood on the floor. Why is she bleeding?"

Erik went to the window and looked. She was right. There was a small pool of blood on the floor next to the chair. He quickly ran to the front door and tried opening it. When his efforts didn't work he stood back and kicked the door, causing it to fly open. Amalie ran into the front room where the girl was sitting in the chair. She was a young woman in her teens with a very sweet face and hair that was golden brown. There was a medical book on the table and a letter.

"Louisa, find the kitchen and bring me some towels."

"Yes, Mother."

Louisa went to the back of the house where she believed the kitchen would be and found some towels but as she turned to exit the kitchen a woman that appeared to be about her mother's age stood in front of her. Her sudden presence startled her and she screamed. Her scream could be heard throughout the house. Erik ran from the front room into the kitchen to investigate. When he reached the kitchen Louisa was sitting under the kitchen table with her face buried in her knees and the woman was trying to reassure her that she wouldn't hurt her.

"Louisa, are you all right?" Erik asked her with concern.

At the sound of her father's voice she bolted from underneath the table and into his arms. Tears were streaming down her face and her heart was racing.

"Everything is fine. I'm sorry I let you come in here by yourself. I should've come with you." He wiped the tears from her eyes and gave her a kiss on her cheek. "Now take the towels to your mother. The young woman needs your help."

"But Father, I'm scared. There may be someone else in the house that I don't know about."

"Young lady, I'm the only other person in this house," the woman reassured Louisa. "You'll be fine. I'm sorry that I startled you."

She scurried off into the front room. The woman began to cough and then sat down in one of the chairs in the kitchen. "I heard you at the door but I don't move too fast these days. I thought Odette was in the house but she must be out."

"I presume that you are Madame Brun."

"Yes, I am and you are?"

"I am Monsieur Geraurd but you may call me Erik. My wife is Doctor Amalie Geraurd. I believe you know the Reverend Troudeaux?"

"Yes, I do."

"It was he who asked my wife to pay you a visit. He said that you were rather ill and in need of a doctor's care."

At that moment it dawned on Madame Brun that he had mentioned a young woman needing help. This alarmed her and she changed the subject quickly from their introductions.

"What has happened to my daughter?"

"My daughter, Louisa, saw her through the window. She was bleeding and motionless. That is why I kicked the door open. I'll repair it as soon as we are certain that she will be all right."

"Odette is hurt?" She began to cry and rose from her chair. "Help me please. I must see her."

He put his arm around her and helped her into the front room. He seated her on one of the small sofas. Amalie had finished wrapping both of her wrists which had stopped the bleeding. She was still unconscious but she didn't understand why. She knew that she had gotten to her in time to help her. Louisa sat by Odette's side rubbing her arm and singing to her as her mother had asked her to do. This helped Louisa keep calm and took Amalie's mind off of the fact that her daughter had just witnessed one of the most horrific things she had ever had to see in her young life.

"What happened here?" Madame Brun asked. "Why are her arms bandaged up?"

Amalie picked up the letter and handed it to Odette's mother. "What is this?"

"We found it on the table next to her medical book," Amalie said as she knelt on the floor next to Odette still massaging her arm to keep the circulation of blood moving.

Madame Brun's tears kept her from seeing the words on the page. She handed the letter to Erik and asked him to read it to her. He obliged. The letter read:

> *Dear Mother,*
> *I know that you have always dreamed of me becoming a doctor but I am just not sure that that is where my heart's desires lie. I know that it is an honorable profession but I find myself dreaming of paints and colors, images and art. Instead of burdening you with disappointment I feel that I must end this charade the only way that I know how. It is because I have not married that you aren't able to afford to seek a doctor's care. Had I not been born with a mark that drives men away you would not have to clothe or feed me and your health would not be failing. Thank you for always loving me just the way I am Mother. I love you and now I will give you my best gift in death.*
> *Love always,*
> *Odette*

The room was quiet. The sadness that filled the letter now filled the room. Madame Brun stood from her chair and Erik helped her to her daughter's side. Amalie moved to allow her to sit next to Odette. Louisa continued to sing and Madame Brun brushed her hair away from her forehead with her fingers so that she could see her face.

"Oh my beautiful daughter, I had no idea that you were burdened so much. I never expected you to cure me. I only wanted you to fulfill *your* dreams."

She leaned over and kissed her forehead. "I love you and no matter what may happen to either of us, as long as we have each other we'll be all right."

Erik kissed Amalie on the forehead as he put his arm around her. "Will she live?"

"I think so. Her cuts weren't deep on her left wrist and they were almost non-existent on the right one. I think we arrived in time. She lost some blood but not enough to cause her to be out as long as she has been. My guess is that she started to cut her wrists and then when she saw the blood she became disoriented. By the time she got to the right wrist, her faculties were not too keen and she passed out from the sight of seeing her own blood."

"Oh, my child….what were you thinking?" Madame Brun cupped her daughter's face in her hand.

"Erik, would you please get my smelling salts from the medical bag? I don't know why I hadn't thought of this earlier."

He picked up the bag and began fumbling through it. He handed her the smelling salts but couldn't help but wonder what was in the small box that was nestled in the bottom of the bag. He had never before seen it there. While Amalie tried to rouse Odette with the salts, he helped himself to a seat on the sofa with the bag perched on his lap. He pulled the box from the bag and opened it. At the sight of the very familiar red stone he couldn't help but wonder how his wife had come to be in possession of this rare gem. Nor could he understand why she had never mentioned it. He would get to the bottom of this mystery but not now. This was not the time or the place. He put the lid back on the box and put it back into her bag.

The young girl began to wake from her stupor and at the sight of her mother's face began to cry. "I'm so sorry Mother. I'm so sorry."

"It's all right child. I had no idea that you felt like such a burden to me. You've never been a burden and you never will be. Do you understand me Odette? I love you and you could never be a disappointment to me."

"Mother, I love you too."

She reached for her mother and embraced her as the tears swept down her cheek and onto her mother's shoulder. "I promise I won't ever try to leave you again." She paused and then sat back in the chair examining the bandages on her wrist. "I'm afraid I wouldn't make a very good doctor, Mother. I couldn't even stand the sight of my own blood. What kind of doctor faints at the sight of their own blood? I'll tell you. A very terrible doctor, that's who."

"It's all right, I never expected you to cure me and I only thought you wanted to become a doctor because you always seemed to enjoy reading the medical books that your grandfather brought you. I hadn't realized that you were so unhappy."

"I only read them because I hoped to find answers as to what illness you have Mother. I would've read anything if I thought it would help and I didn't want to be rude to Grandfather. He's always been so sweet and tried so hard to be the father that I never knew." She smiled at her mother as she held her hand.

"Odette, if your dreams lie elsewhere, then I want you to follow them. However, I don't want you to ever believe that you're a burden to me. I would gladly give my life to save yours. You're my daughter and I love you. And apparently God has heard our prayers since Doctor Geraurd is here now." She looked over at Amalie and smiled. "I'd say we've both been blessed today by her presence. If she hadn't shown up when she did I may be mourning yet another family member's untimely demise." Tears rolled down her cheeks as she kissed Odette's hand.

Amalie walked over to Madame Brun and put her hand on her shoulder. "Madame Brun, I think it's probably wise that we get you to your room so that you may rest and that I might have time to examine you."

"Certainly, my dear but please don't call me Madame Brun, my name is Claire and I'd be more comfortable if we weren't so formal. After all, we're practically family since you saved my daughter's life."

"Your daughter wouldn't have died Madame....I mean Claire. She didn't lose enough blood and the cut had already started to clot before I got to her. However, I'm glad that I was here to help."

"Nevertheless, you're a kind woman and you sought to help a total stranger without thought."

"I will honor your wishes and now I must get you where I can examine you. Time is critical now. The Reverend said that you've been ill for several weeks now." She turned and looked at Erik. "Would you mind bringing my bag?"

"I'm right behind you my love. Louisa, stay here with Odette and get her anything she needs."

"Yes Father."

Amalie helped Claire to her feet and walked slowly with her to her room. She put her into her bed and made her comfortable. Then she took her bag from Erik and began her examination. Erik left the room and joined Odette and Louisa. After making sure that they were all right, he decided to do an examination of his own. He went to the door he had kicked and looked over the damage to the door and its frame. He concluded that it would require reconstruction.

"Odette, do you have any tools for building in your stable?" he asked as he continued to look at the tattered edges of the door frame.

"I'm not sure we have anything for building but I know that Grandfather does. His house is up the road, over the other side of the hill. He's not home right now but I'm sure he wouldn't mind if you borrowed his tools."

"I'm sure that he wouldn't had he met me first but I'm not going onto his property without his knowledge. I'll go into the village and get the lumber that I need to repair the door and hopefully he will be home when I get back."

"He doesn't usually get home until close to supper time but he always comes by our house first before he goes home. You may ask him then."

Odette's smile lit the room. It was good to see her so positive after she had tried to take her life. It made him realize that they had definitely done the right thing coming to help this family. After all of the years living in such darkness and doubting his own purpose, he was beginning to truly see that God definitely had a larger purpose for him and his family. Not just the purpose of loving each other but passing that love onto those that needed their talents and skills.

He went to the door of Claire's room and knocked lightly. Amalie opened the door and inquired, "Yes, Erik what is it?"

"I'm going to go into the village to get some lumber to fix the door. I'll return in a couple of hours. I'm sure you'll be fine here."

"That's fine. Would you mind picking up a few things for me from the local apothecary? I believe that Claire has an inflammation of her bronchial tubes and if I were to get her the proper treatment I should be able to get it under control. If you wouldn't mind acquiring some Syrup of Squills and Nitrate of Potash from the apothecary I believe I have everything else I require in my medical bag. Also, Claire has requested, quite strongly that we stay here until it is time for us to make our way home."

He looked into her brown eyes and knew that saying no to her request was not an option. He knew that she would feel better being closer to her patient just in case she needed her and he was happy to oblige.

"I'll get our things from the inn when I'm there. It may take me a bit longer to return but I'll do my best to be back quickly."

She kissed his cheek. "Thank you and please be careful."

He turned and exited the hallway, entering the room where he had left Louisa talking with Odette. He stood quietly in the doorway listening to their conversation. As a parent he had always wondered how his daughter would do in a social setting among people she didn't know. So, he took this opportunity to observe her. He noticed how well she listened to Odette speak and how very considerate of her feelings she was; never once referring to her in a manner that was rude or judgmental considering all that she had seen and heard.

"Odette, I'm glad that we came to your house. I'm sorry that you got hurt but my mother was able to help you. Are you feeling better now?"

"Yes, Louisa. I am." She smiled at her and then put her hand on her cheek. "How old are you Louisa?

"I'm six years old and I won't be seven until next spring. At least that is what Mother always tells me. How old are you Odette?"

"I just had my eighteenth birthday last week."

Louisa leaned closer to her and asked with a grin on her face, "Did you have a cake and presents?"

"Unfortunately Louisa, my mother was too ill to bake me a cake and all the money we have has been put away to pay for a doctor to come help Mother." She looked at Louisa as her cheerful face turned into a face of sadness.

"I'm sure that my mother will let you keep some of the money so that you can buy a nice present for yourself. She's always doing nice things for people."

She looked into Louisa's blue eyes and then put her hand on her shoulder. "If your mother can help my mother then I'll be glad to give her all of the money we have put away. The only thing I wished for on my birthday was that my mother was well again."

"I'm sure my mother can help her get better, just like she helped you."

"Yes, Louisa, she did help me and I'm glad that she did or we wouldn't be friends. My wrists are only a part of what needs healing on me," she mumbled just loud enough for her new friend to hear her.

"What do you mean? Are you sick too?"

She could see the worry in the young girls face and answered her quickly.

"No, I'm not ill."

"Then why do you need my mother's help?"

"Can you keep a secret, Louisa?" Odette had never thought she would ever share what she was about to reveal but for some reason the words came without effort or even fear.

"Yes, I can keep a secret. My father tells me secrets all of the time and I haven't told anyone."

"All right, I'll tell you. Are you ready?"

She nodded and then Odette pulled her long hair off of the back of her neck, pulling it up so that she could see her secret. From the back of her left ear, down her neck to her shoulder her skin was reddish and had raised bumps. Her left ear was smaller than most ears and a portion of the lobe was deformed.

Louisa stood next to her, looking at her secret. She wanted to touch it but didn't because she didn't want to upset Odette. "It's amazing!"

"It's disgusting, is what it is," scowled Odette.

"No, it's not. It looks like my father's head. He has the same red skin and bumps that you have. It's wonderful."

Erik, still in the door way, listened as his sweet daughter told her new friend how wonderful her birthmark was. She didn't know that she was supposed to be repulsed or even frightened by such a sight. It was normal to her and Erik knew all too well how she had wished she also had a face like his. He thought about interrupting her but decided to see how far she would take the conversation. He decided he would observe a little longer before interrupting them. However, he was very surprised to see that someone else had a similar mark as he. Fortunately, hers was easily concealed and undetectable to prying eyes.

"How can you say that it's wonderful? Look at me. I look like a monster."

"No, Odette, you're beautiful and so is your birthmark. God gave it to you and He knows what He is doing. He gave my father his too. And do you want to know why He gave it to him?"

"Yes, Louisa. I would *love* to know why He gave it to him."

"Father said that God made his face that way so that Mother would be able to find him and I believe him."

"And why do you believe him?"

"Because Mother found him didn't she?"

At the time that Odette was about to answer, Erik walked into the room and said, "Yes, she did. She found me *and* she married me." He picked up Louisa and kissed her. "Only God can explain why but she did and now I have a wonderful family."

"Is that why you wear the mask Monsieur Geraurd?"

"Yes, mademoiselle, that is why I wear it. It is much more terrifying than anything you may show me. You're a beautiful young woman and somewhere out there, there is a man that will love you just as you are."

The frown that had been on her face suddenly turned to a smile. No one other than her mother and grandfather had ever paid her such a wonderful compliment about her appearance.

"Thank you, Monsieur Geraurd but I really don't think anyone will ever want to marry me."

"I used to think that too, but as you can see I was wrong. When the time is right, you too shall find that one person that makes everything seem possible." He kissed Louisa again and set her down. "I have to go into the village to get a few things to fix the door and for your mother. Also, Madame Brun has insisted that we stay here for the duration of our visit, so I'll be getting our things from the inn also."

"Did you hear that, Odette? We're going to be staying here with you." She ran over to her new friend and gave her a hug. "We're going to have so much fun."

"Louisa, don't tire her out. She needs to rest too."

"It's all right Monsieur Geraurd. She's no bother and I'm feeling better. It'll be nice to have some company."

"If you need anything, your mother is down the hall."

Erik smiled at them both and then exited the house.

You Again

When Erik returned from his trip into the village the sun was making its descent among the trees. He had to retain the use of a wagon in order to bring back the lumber along with their luggage from the inn. The coach that had been provided to them by the Reverend was left behind in Etrepagny along with its driver. He had given the coachman their room at the inn and told him to use it as long as they were there. He also told him that he would send for him when it was time to return to Trie-Chateau. He came to the front door with luggage in hand. He set it on the front stoop and then returned for another load. When all of their belongings had been brought to the house, he knocked on the tattered door and waited for someone to open it.

Odette came to the door and slowly pulled it open. "Come in Monsieur. I'm so glad that you made it back before Grandfather came by the house." She noticed the luggage that was sitting outside of her front door. "Are all of these yours?"

"Yes they are. Well, some of them are mine. Most of them are Doctor Geraurd's. I've never known a woman to travel with less than what she needs." He smiled a crooked smile and then rolled his eyes.

"Father, you've returned." Louisa had joined them outside as they began picking up the luggage to bring it inside the house. "May I help?"

"Of course you may help." He pointed to the left of her. "You may bring that small bag sitting over there. I believe that is full of your things."

She skipped over to the bag and struggled to pick it up but succeeded.

"Where shall we put them Odette?"

"I believe Mother has decided that you'll have the room at the end of the hall past the dining room. Louisa will share my room if that is all right with you and Doctor Geraurd?"

"That will be fine as long as it's not an imposition."

"Of course not, I always wanted a little sister and now I'll have one, at least for a few days, anyway. It'll be fun."

After making several trips they completed the task of transferring the luggage to their respective rooms.

"Where is your mother?" he asked Louisa.

"She's in the kitchen making supper and Madame Brun is resting."

He went to the kitchen where he found Amalie cooking a large pot of stew over a hot stove and the aroma of bread wafted across the room causing his mouth to water.

"It smells wonderful."

"Thank you. Did you bring the items I asked for from the apothecary?"

"Yes, they're sitting on the dresser in our room. How is your patient feeling?"

"The initial treatment seems to be helping but I wanted to make sure that I had something stronger to give to her to help aid in the expelling of the mucus that has clogged her bronchial tubes. We should be able to see some progress in the next couple of days or so. She's very strong willed which helps."

He leaned over and kissed her on the cheek as she stirred the stew. "Just like someone else I know."

"Yes, and it's a good thing that I am or you wouldn't be standing here." Amalie took the pot of stew off of the fire and put the lid on it. She gently touched Erik's arm, moving him out of her way so that she could look inside the oven to see if the bread was done.

"I owe all of my good fortune to you my love, I won't deny that. However, your stubbornness isn't always rewarding."

"We can discuss my stubborn nature at another date. At the moment I would like for you to ask the girls to come set the table while I get Claire ready for supper."

"And what is it that you would like for me to do?"

"You may start a fire in the fireplace in the sitting room. The warmer air will help to clear her lungs."

Erik found the girls and told them of Amalie's request for help in the kitchen. He then exited the house through the back entrance to find the wood for the fire he was to build. As he made his way to the stable he was greeted with the sound of the hammer of a revolver being readied to be fired at him.

"Stop where you are Monsieur," a gruff, older but familiar voice shouted. Erik stopped walking, putting his hands out where they could be seen. As he started to turn to face the man the voice said, "Move slowly."

He did as he was told and as Erik's eyes locked in on the old man's face he let out a sigh of relief. "I believe I know you sir."

"I don't think so. I don't know anyone who would set a foot on my land without my permission."

"This is your land?"

"Yes, and you're not welcome on it."

"I can't believe that you don't recognize me from this morning."

"What happened this morning?"

"I was eating at the café where you are employed and you asked me and my family to leave. Don't you remember?"

The old man walked a little closer to him so that he could get a better look at him, lowering his revolver slightly. He looked at Erik's face and then the rest of him.

"Yes, I remember now. I insulted you and you gave me twice the amount of what was owed for your meal. You are a strange fellow but that doesn't tell me why you are on my land."

There was a moment of awkward silence and then Erik spoke kindly to the man, trying to persuade him away from any notions that he might have about pulling the trigger of his revolver.

"Sir, if you don't mind I'd be more comfortable if you would put your revolver away. I plan to do you no harm. I am here with my wife and daughter. My name is Monsieur Erik Geraurd and my wife is Dr. Amalie Geraurd. We were asked to come here to help Madame Brun by the Reverend Troudeaux who lives in Trie-Chateau. I was going to the stable to retrieve firewood for the fire."

The older gentleman held his revolver steady continuing to aim at Erik. "Reverend Troudeaux?" How do I know you aren't lying to me?"

"You don't but I'm asking you to trust me."

"How do you know Henry?"

"He's the Reverend at the small church I attend in Trie-Chateau. I would even go so far as to say he was a very good friend of mine."

"He's never mentioned you. What did you say your wife's name was?"

"Dr. Amalie Geraurd."

"Her name sounds familiar. Henry mentioned that she might be able to help but wasn't sure she would come."

"Well, she has come and she is with Madame Brun right now. I promise I'm not going to hurt you. Please, lower your revolver and let me get the firewood. You're welcome to keep an eye on me if you like but I must get the firewood."

After a few seconds and some thought Remy lowered his revolver.

"You seem harmless enough but I'm going to come with you. I'm sorry that I drew my weapon on you but we don't get very many visitors out here and I wasn't aware that my cousin Henry had sent anyone to help us."

"It's quite alright Monsieur. You're protecting you family and what is yours. I would have done the same. Now let's go get that firewood before they start to wonder what has happened to me."

Remy laughed a hearty laugh then walked slowly beside Erik as they made their way to the stable.

"Where are my manners, I'm Monsieur Remy Brun but you may call me Remy. I'm Claire's father-in-law."

"I assumed as much from what Odette told me. She said you would be home around supper time."

They continued to talk as they loaded a small wheelbarrow full of wood to transport to the house. He informed Remy that his daughter-in-law's condition would soon be improving and then explained to him the condition of the front door and what had happened with his grand-daughter. This bit of news saddened Remy. Erik suggested that he not make too much of the earlier incident. She seemed to be doing well and it may upset her. Remy agreed. Sometimes the best thing to do or say is nothing at all.

When they reached the house they entered through the back entrance and made their way into the sitting room where the fireplace was located. Remy stacked the wood inside the fireplace on top of the kindling and then Erik used his homemade flint lighter to start the fire quickly. The two men sat in the sitting room talking until they saw Amalie enter the room with Claire at her side.

Remy rose to his feet and then greeted Claire with a kiss on the cheek. "You are looking much better already, my dear."

"Yes and I'm feeling better too. I am so grateful for the new friends we have here at our house and Cousin Henry for sending them. He's always been such a great help to us ever since Thomas and little Edmond passed."

Remy took her arm and helped walk her to the dining room where the girls had set a beautiful table. They all took their seats, said a blessing to thank God for the meal and then began eating.

After supper, the girls cleared and washed the dishes while the adults retired to the sitting room for tea and dessert. The girls joined them after their chores were done. They sat quietly in the corner crocheting and doing needlepoint. On occasion you could hear them whispering and giggling together.

"It's so wonderful to see Odette enjoying herself again. It's been months since I've heard her laugh like that." Claire said as she finished taking a sip of tea.

"Yes, Louisa is very good at making people laugh. I think God gave her an extra dose of humor when He made her," Erik said as he tended the fire.

"Humor is something we all need a bit more of these days. Life has been too tragic……. and sad these……..past years," Claire said as she coughed between words.

Remy held Claire's hand and said, "Yes but I think our luck may be changing."

"I think you're right. God has sent us angels to care for us."

"Dr. Geraurd, no matter the cost, we'll do whatever we can to repay our debt to you. We have been saving a very long time." Remy pulled some money from his pocket.

Amalie glanced at Erik and he returned the look and then walked over to Remy.

"Put your money away, friend. Your bill has been paid already."

"Who has paid it?"

"You have," Erik said with a smile.

"And how did I do that? I've given you no money."

"You've paid with your hospitality towards my family and with the love you have for your own family. No money is required when we are doing simply what love has called us to do."

"But I must pay you something, it wouldn't be right."

"What wouldn't be right is for you to insult me by insisting on paying. So, please consider your debt paid and I'll hear no more about it."

"I can see that arguing with you is futile so I'll succumb to your wishes but someday you'll let me do for you what you have done for me."

"No, Remy, someday I hope that you will do for someone else that which I have done for you. It was the kindness of your cousin Henry that allowed me to continue to make a life for myself within the village of Trie-Chateau. It was his kindness that I now pass onto you. Now you must pass our kindness on to someone else. That is how God wants us to live, is it not?"

"I would like to hear how Henry helped you. Would you mind telling me the story?"

Erik sat down on the hearth and began telling the events of his life that had happened after he had met Amalie. He told them about the first time he met Reverend Troudeaux and how he was surprised that he made no comment about his face being covered by a mask. It was as if he never noticed it at all. He treated him with respect from the first time he had ever spoken to him and always defended him against those that didn't quite see him as a person. He was a unique person in many ways and it was comforting to have him as his friend.

When he finished his story, Amalie asked Odette to help Louisa get ready for bed and she helped Claire to her room where she gave her more of the medicine she had prepared for her. She then said good night to the girls and informed Erik that she would be retiring too. She opened the door to the room in which they were to stay and was glad to see that Erik had taken the liberty of unpacking her items, placing them in the wardrobe. She was thankful that her husband had not been swayed by the societal rules that would have prevented him from doing what most men would assume to be the duties of a woman. She noted that he had always done what he could to help her and that was part of the attraction she had for him. He didn't always tell her that he loved her but his actions always conveyed the message for him.

She changed into her night dress and then sat at the dressing table to brush her hair. The room was dimly lit with lamps fueled by kerosene which made a warm glow around the room. As she brushed her hair she noticed a drawing of a man hanging on the wall. It probably would have gone unnoticed except that the small lamp beside the bed cast a light that illuminated it, creating a spotlight that awakened the face in the frame like the sun awakens a sleeping bloom. There was something about the face that seemed familiar. She rose from the dressing table and walked over to the drawing to get a better look. The hair was different but the jaw line, the cheeks and the eyes were very similar to a face she knew she had seen before now. She tried to remember where she had seen the face but she couldn't quite place it. Perhaps if she got some rest it would come to her. After all it had been a very busy day and she was exhausted not only physically but mentally. She turned the lamp down, climbed into bed and immediately after she shut her eyes she fell asleep.

In the sitting room Erik and Remy continued talking and getting to know each other. Remy told him about the day that his son and grandson were murdered. After hearing the circumstances surrounding this tragic event, Erik knew why Remy had never once commented about his appearance. His grandson had been born with a similar disfigurement to the left side of his face as his own. The child was blind in his left eye and could only hear out of his right ear. His skin was reddish in color and it was as if it were swollen from the top of his forehead to his chin. His nose, however, was perfectly placed on his face.

"It sounds like your grandson was born with a face much like my own."

"Your mask covers it well." Remy gave his mask a quick look, touching it lightly with his hand to feel the texture of it.

"Yes, but it is the mask that makes strangers assume the very worst of me."

"Erik, I wouldn't normally ask and I'm sure that you're a private man but would you mind showing me your face?"

Erik thought for a moment knowing that over six years ago he wouldn't have ever entertained the idea of letting someone he had just met see what he hid behind his mask. It was strange but he understood why his companion wanted to see it. He slowly untied the strap that held it in place and removed it from his face.

"Is it what you expected?" Erik asked.

"I'm not sure what you mean."

"Is it just as unbelievable a sight as the face your grandson bore?"

"The sight of it isn't so unbelievable since I have seen someone's face that was so similar. What is unbelievable, if you'll pardon my manners, is that you have managed to stay alive as long as you have."

Erik placed the mask back onto his face and replied, "Unbelievable is not the word I would use. Miraculous is more like it. My life has been a journey that I wouldn't wish on anyone but it was worth it to finally get to where I am today."

"And where is that Erik?"

"I'm where God intended me to be all of the time. I'm happy and I have a family that extends beyond my wife and child. I can't say that I honestly understand all that has been allowed to happen to me but as the scriptures read we are to consider all things joy."

"Are you saying that I'm to consider the murder of my child and grandson joy?"

"Of course I'm not! A life that is taken is never something that any-one should consider joy. I believe the joy comes from finding it in your heart to continue to love those that are no longer with you. You should try to honor their memory by giving to others what those that took from you could not find it in themselves to give.......understanding and forgiveness."

Remy gave him a look of disbelief and became quite angry. "I'm supposed to find understanding and forgiveness for murderers? Are you mad?" His voice rose in a thunderous cloud enveloping the room.

"No, Remy, I am quite sane. It has been my experience that hating does nothing to a man's soul except keep it from reaching its fullest potential. What harm does a man do to another man by hating him? Does the man you hate know or care that you do? I don't think he does. So, while you brood and hate a man who doesn't care or know that you hate him, you relive your pain every day by keeping the hate alive and he continues on with his life unaffected by your hate. Your son was an honorable man who loved his child and died while defending his right to have a life no matter what he looked like. Your grandson was a young child who was caught up by the society that teaches prejudice against things it doesn't understand or can't repair. Thomas and Edmond Brun will always have a purpose in this life and that is to remind the rest of us that we shouldn't judge anyone by their appearance and that another person's right to life is worth dying for no matter the circumstances. You have much to be joyful about when you understand that they have taught a lesson and that lesson can only be taught to others by those who witnessed it first-hand. That is how people's lives are changed Remy; by sharing in the sorrow and joys of others."

His words flooded Remy's ears and tears began to run down his cheek. He knew that Erik was right and that continuing to carry the anger and resentment around with him would no longer serve him. He held his head in his hands trying to hide his emotions. Erik stood and walked to where he was seated and sat next to him, putting his hand on his shoulder.

"It's all right, Remy. No one knows your pain as well as I. It took the majority of my life to finally realize that hating what I couldn't change was never going to set me free. I wasted a lot of years being angry at people that didn't even know I existed nor did they care."

Remy raised his head as he wiped the tears from his eyes with his handkerchief. "I never realized that I had been hanging onto the anger until your words pierced my ears and opened my heart to the truth. I'm a wretched man with nothing but bitterness and distrust in my heart. It's too late for me to change…..too many years have been taken away from me already."

"It's not too late my friend. It's never too late to do what God has asked you to do."

"And what is that Erik….what is it that He is asking me to do?"

"Forgive not just those that have wronged you but to trust that He will be there to help you through it. We aren't perfect men Remy and we never will be. It's only when we come to accept our limitations as men that we truly begin to understand that God is the only way that we'll ever reach or stand in the face of perfection. Amalie's father told me many years ago that we are just men that have been given a task by God…..we either choose to do it or we don't but we will live with the consequences of denying him. I didn't understand what he meant until years later but when God was ready to bring me to that understanding and I allowed Him to do so, it was as if a fog had been lifted from my eyes."

"I'm not sure that I can forgive those men. They don't deserve my forgiveness."

"Neither did I Remy."

He looked at Erik with a puzzled expression upon his face not understanding what he had said. "What are you speaking of Erik. You're no murderer."

Erik thought for a moment. He wanted to share his story without alarming his new friend. He knew it would be risky but something inside compelled him to tell him what his life had been like. He wanted to show how drastically he had changed but only because others chose to forgive and understand. He walked slowly to the fireplace, stirring the almost smoldering embers.

"I would appear not to be but then again appearances can be quite deceiving. You don't have a face like mine and never come to a crossroads at some point when you have to choose between saving your own life by taking another's."

The surprise and disappointment on Remy's face was noticeable. The shock of Erik's statement rendered him unable to verbalize his thoughts. All he could do was sit and think about what he was capable of and if he'd try to hurt him if he questioned him.

"You're surprised. I can see it on your face. You're also wondering if I will harm you and your family. The answer is no." He walked back over to the chair where he had been sitting and sat down.

"You see, it's not so much what I did but why I had to do it. Kill or be killed. Your son and grandson would have understood that, just as I believe you do now. I took no pleasure in what I did. No, it didn't make it right and I'll forever regret not making a different decision on how to handle those situations but I can't change it."

"Does your wife know about your indiscretions?" Remy interjected.

"Yes, she does."

"Then how could she possibly love you?"

"Forgiveness and understanding, that's how she can love me or anyone else that has done something that is believed to have been so irreparable. I'm thankful every day that God has allowed her to have that capacity in which to love me."

Remy sat with his head in hands once again.

"I don't understand the reason you are telling me all of this. How is this supposed to help me forgive anyone? You're obviously not who you say you are and...."

"But I am who I say I am. Just because you're opinion of me is now jaded due to my confession of what I have done in my past doesn't mean that I'm not who I say I am. Aren't we all a product of our past actions and experiences as well as our present? You can't honestly sit there and tell me that you've never done one thing in your life that would cause someone to question who you truly are? I would have to say that you are a liar if you did. The person that stands before you today could not and would not have ever come into existence had someone not forgiven me and given me the opportunity to change."

"But some people don't ever change and don't want to change," Remy interrupted.

"Yes, you're right but how would you ever know that unless you gave them that opportunity? The reason most people don't change is because they aren't given that opportunity. Most people assume that once a man is condemned he should remain condemned." Erik shifted his position in his seat, leaning toward his companion.

"My wife's father believed that good is present in everyone. He believed that although at times it seems to be absent, if you just look for it you can usually find it. He saw it in me even when I didn't see it in myself. It was his grace and openness to me that changed my life. His daughter, my wife, saw it even after she knew about everything that was in my past. She forgave me not because I deserved it but because she was willing to believe as her father did. She wanted to give me the opportunity to change and the freedom to make mistakes while trying to do so. I'm not saying that you should forget what they did but at least try to forgive them because it was their ignorance and fear that drove them to their hate and we're all susceptible to those things."

"They murdered them for no reason Erik. They slaughtered them like livestock in the streets and all because of his face. To me that is unforgiveable." His sobs almost made his words inaudible.

"And to God every sin we commit is unforgiveable and yet He *does* forgive us. Are you better than God that you should pass judgment on men that He himself forgives? Judgment is not for mortals to pass, that is left for God to decide and I'm grateful for that or I wouldn't have the loving family that I have."

"I still don't know if I can forgive them or you for misrepresenting yourself."

"I haven't done anything of the kind. I'm merely a man that has a past and has done well to free myself of it most days. I had hoped you wouldn't hold it against me but if you choose to I can't stop you from doing so. I suppose I should have expected your reaction to be one of fear since that is obviously why you can't forgive or let go of the past."

"How dare you accuse me of such a thing? I'm not afraid to forgive."

"Oh but aren't you? You're afraid that if you forgive these treacherous men that it somehow diminishes the life of your son and grandson. And then if you don't hang onto your anger, bitterness and resentment you're afraid that you'll eventually forget Thomas and Edmond. Fear is a catalyst to many decisions we make or choose not to make it. It is courage that you need to have now; courage to face that fear and to trust not in what *you* are able to handle but what you are willing to let *God* handle for you."

"You make it sound like it's easy."

"It's anything *but* easy Remy. However, once you've freed yourself of that burden your life will never be the same."

"Sure, it's easy for you to say that because you were the receiver of forgiveness. I would like to hear what your wife has to say about it. And not just her but the families of the people that you murdered or do they even know it was you?"

"I can see that you're trying hard to make sense of the fact that someone you deem so despicable is sitting before you asking you to do something that you don't believe I have any right to ask you to do. I can't make you understand it. I'm not sure that I understand it myself. It wasn't until sixteen years after Amalie's father spoke to me about God and his capacity to forgive me for all that I had done that I even recognized I needed forgiveness or that I needed to forgive those that I believed to have wronged me."

Remy looked at Erik with distrust in his eyes. He had never met anyone who was so convicted about his beliefs. It made no sense that he would put himself in a bad light when the repercussions could be so costly.

"You still haven't answered my questions?"

"Does it matter if they knew it was me? Would knowing who took their family member's life change the fact that they are no longer living?"

"No. But at least you would be jailed or even better, you would be dead?"

"Locking me up would solve what problem? Would killing me bring them back? You have judged me without even knowing the other person's part in the situation. Had I not defended myself against the evils of men like the ones that killed your son and grandson, I wouldn't be here now with my wife helping your daughter-in-law and grand-daughter. Every story has two sides Remy and not every side is as black and white as you would like it to be."

"What do you mean?"

"Well, what would have happened if your son would have killed the two men that had killed him? What would you have said about your son then? Would his actions have been justified or would you have condemned him too?"

"It's not the same. If he had killed them it would have been because he was protecting his family."

"But murder is murder and no one person's life is to be thought more important than another." Erik taunted him with his words.

"But there are evil people in this world that kill for no reason. They would deserve to die."

"So having a reason makes it justifiable? Oh Remy, you have just announced that I am innocent of my crimes with that assumption."

"I did what?"

"Reason or no reason, I will always be accountable for the things that I have done. No matter what my punishment here on Earth, it will not erase what I have done or heal those that I have hurt. I can only pray that God will have mercy on my soul and hope that those around me will judge me for who I am *now* and not for the mistakes I have made in the past. I would hope that you would be able to do that for me too Remy since I have not judged you by your actions earlier today at the café."

Remy's red, tear-filled eyes starred quietly at the floor. He knew in his heart that Erik wasn't a monster. Although he didn't want to willingly forgive the men that had taken his son and grandson from him, he also knew that it was time to rid himself of his anger and hate.

"Erik, I'm not quite sure why our paths have crossed but I do know one thing with great certainty."

"And what is that my friend?"

"God has his own ways of showing us our faults and convicting us of our own self-righteousness. I would've never believed that someone such as you could have ever convinced me that a condemned man deserved my forgiveness much less that I would feel compelled to grant it."

"We are *all* condemned men if we don't seek God's forgiveness and that is why we must show compassion and understanding to one another, even when we don't believe it is deserved. It is out of a man's compassion and forgiveness that others are allowed to better themselves and are able to begin to turn away from their wickedness. Without opportunities there are no successes and a man's failures are all he will ever have to cling to in his life."

"I'm glad that my cousin Henry sent you here. Henry has tried to speak to me about this for years and I turned my ear from his words. And then you came here; a very unlikely messenger for me to listen to indeed."

Remy chuckled and then stood up from his seat. He put his hand on Erik's shoulder. "When they say that the Lord works in mysterious ways, they were obviously referring to you."

Erik laughed along with him and then replied, "Yes, I agree. I'm as mysterious as they come and I still have yet to figure out why He has chosen me, the most unlikely of souls to share His message."

"I don't know either but I'm glad He has." He smiled at him and then started to walk toward the front door that was mangled from the day's earlier event. As he opened the door to exit he turned to him and said, "Thank you for reminding me of who I am supposed to be. My heart is burdened less tonight and I'll sleep better than I have in years."

"You're welcome Remy. I'll see you in the morning."

Erik shut the door behind him and then made his way into the bedroom where Amalie lay sleeping. She was beautiful while she slept. He changed into his night shirt and slipped under the covers, pulled her close to him and kissed her gently on her delicate lips. "Good night my love," he whispered.

Recognition

$\mathcal{T}$he next couple of days were spent tending to Claire's needs and repairing the door. Louisa and Odette had become inseparable. They would help Amalie with the chores during the morning but during the afternoons Odette would help Louisa with her studies. She was a very good tutor and Erik noticed how well his daughter received the lessons from her.

"You are a wonderful teacher, Odette," he complimented her as he observed her interacting with Louisa.

"Thank you Monsieur Geraurd. Louisa makes it very easy to teach since she is interested in learning. I have tutored many children that had no interest in knowledge at all and I didn't think they would ever learn."

"Did they?"

"Yes, but it required a lot more work from me than them."

"Then I would say that you were a successful teacher. Knowledge is its own reward and it's obvious that you understand that. If you are able to pass that along to others then you have been successful. I will let you continue with your studies."

He exited the room and made his way into the kitchen where Amalie was preparing an herbal drink for Claire. He sat down at the table and began going through her medical bag looking for the box with the gem. Amalie turned around to find him fumbling through her bag.

"What are you looking for Erik?" she asked with an agitated voice.

He continued to rummage through the items in the bag without answering her. Then he pulled out the box, opened it and examined the contents by holding it up where the light could catch the cut edges; showing its beauty as the light passed through it.

"This is what I am looking for my love." He continued to marvel at it.

"Why are you looking for that?"

"Actually, a better question would be why didn't you tell me that you had such a wonderful gem? Where *did* you get such a beautiful diamond?"

Amalie felt the color drain from her face. She hadn't meant to keep the gem a secret but it was clear that she had and now she would have to explain.

"It was a gift from Hessam many years ago. Remember when they stayed in the cave after we were married before everything happened with Frederic?"

"Yes, go on. I'm listening." Erik sat staring at her with a smug look on his face. He already knew where it had come from but it was fun hearing his wife explain her omission of its existence.

"He gave it to me that afternoon. He told me that you had given it to him as a gift for sparing his life. And since I had done the same, he felt that it was appropriate to give it to me. I believe his words were, 'I may have been the rarest of gems Erik had laid eyes on then but you, Amalie are the rarest gem of all."

"That sounds like something the Persian would have said."

"I'm sorry that I never showed it to you Erik but you know how quickly things escalated with Frederic and then the baby. I put it away and truly forgot about it until we were on our way here. I had gone to my jewelry box to get my wedding ring and there it was. I thought perhaps I would have it made into a ring or necklace while we were here."

"Oh no my love, this gem will stay as it is."

"Why is that?"

"Let's just say that it's not something that was meant to be shown to the whole world. It has a purpose and a past that is only meant to be shared among friends. You haven't shown it to anyone else have you?"

"No, I haven't."

"Good. I will keep it with me and I will definitely be having a conversation with the Persian once we return home."

"Erik, you're starting to scare me with the way you are speaking about this stone. What possible reason could you have for keeping it a secret?"

"It's best that you don't know Amalie. The important thing is that I find a way to rid us of this wretched diamond."

"I'm your wife Erik and I demand to know what this is all about." Her frustration and worry was evident in her tone.

He gently grabbed her by the arms and looked lovingly in her eyes.

"I'll tell you in time Amalie. I don't like keeping things from you but at this moment it's best that you don't know any more than what the Persian has told you. Once we return home and I've had time to think about things I promise I'll tell you everything I know about this gem." He kissed her on the forehead and embraced her. "Now, I think you need to give Claire her drink before it gets cold."

"I'll trust you but as soon as we get home I want answers."

"You'll get them. I promise."

She put the cup on a saucer and then exited the room. Erik put the diamond in a small leather pouch he kept with him and then returned the pouch to his pocket. It would be safe as long as it was with him. He didn't understand why the Persian wanted to rid himself of it and why after all these years he had decided to do so. It made no sense to him.

Amalie entered the room where Claire was resting. She handed her the cup and then sat in a chair that was next to the bed.

"How is it?"

"It's good. I'm feeling much better. I'm so grateful for your help Amalie. I truly thought I would not survive this."

"You're strong Claire and although you may have become weakened, I think you would have recovered."

"Maybe, but I'm still glad you came. It's been so long since I have had another woman to speak with about my life. I love Odette but she is still a child and I don't like burdening her with my problems."

"I'm also glad that we came. It's been nice to visit a new place and see new things."

"Is your room adequate? If you need more blankets ask Odette to get them for you. I know that the evenings can get cold in this old house."

"The room is very accommodating and we're very comfortable. You have a very beautiful home Claire." She rose from her chair and began looking at some of the photographs that were hanging on the wall.

"Claire, the drawing of the man that hangs above the bed in the room in which I am staying....who is he?"

"It was Thomas' grandmother's father, his name was Jean Troudeaux. I don't know much about him other than he was loved by his family and was a stone mason until the day he died."

"His face seemed very familiar to me but he doesn't look anything like Reverend Troudeaux."

"You're right about that. I think Cousin Henry favors his mother's side of the family. However, his sister's son, Charles Rousseau looks exactly like him."

"Did you say Charles Rousseau?"

"Yes. Do you know him?"

"I know a Chester Rousseau but not a Charles Rousseau."

"That's him. He stopped using the name Charles many years ago. He had a friend by the name of Gaston Girault that thought he was quite entertaining and nicknamed him Charles the Jester. From what I've been told they were thicker than thieves. Later he combined the names and just called him Chester. It's silly really but it did seem to fit him better than his given name."

"Monsieur Girault was my father. I don't recall him ever telling me that story and neither has Chester."

"Your father was quite a man Amalie. He was closer than a brother to Chester."

"Yes, I know."

"I don't think you do."

"What do you mean?"

"Apparently there was some event early in their lives that bonded them together. No one ever spoke about it publicly but the whispers were always heard."

"Do you know what the event was?"

"The only thing that I had heard was that it had something to do with a young woman that Chester had fallen in love with when he was only nineteen. Apparently she was married. Anything I would tell you after that would be strictly speculation and rumor and I don't think that Chester deserves to be the subject of my assumptions. He's a good man and that's all I've ever needed to know."

"I agree Claire and who among us hasn't had something in our past that may have raised an eyebrow or two?"

They looked at each other and smiled. Then simultaneously they said, "Not me," and then burst into laughter.

"Oh Amalie, it is so wonderful to laugh again. This house has been so quiet. It's almost as if life had ceased to exist here."

"I'm grateful to be a part of your life Claire. I hope that we will always remain friends. Now I think you need to get some rest before supper, so I'll close the drapes and let you sleep."

She closed the drapes and exited the room, gently pulling the door shut. She walked to the room where they were staying and sat on the dressing table stool facing the portrait on the wall. Now her curiosity was peaked. What had happened between her father and Chester that put them on their path to such a long and vital friendship? She knew she should put it out of her head but there was still something about that drawing on the wall that reminded her of someone and it wasn't Chester. She had known him for a long time but she hadn't seen him when he was the age of the man in the drawing so she knew it couldn't be him that it reminded her of now. It would come to her if she stopped obsessing over it and as soon as she was home, she would ask Chester about what she had learned. She was surprised that neither the Reverend nor Chester had ever mentioned being related to each other. That seemed very odd to her. Why wouldn't they have made it known?

If Chester's mother was the Reverend's sister, then that would make Chester his nephew. This was developing into an even bigger mystery than she thought. Thinking about all of the family connections made her begin to wonder about Erik's family. The only thing she knew about his mother was that she despised him because of his appearance and he had never spoken much about his father.

Erik entered the room. "How is your patient?"

"She's resting now but I can see that she will make a full recovery."

"Then why do you look so disappointed?"

She pointed to the portrait of the man on the wall. "This is Chester's great grandfather. Were you aware that Chester is the Reverend Troudeaux's nephew?"

"No, but you're acting like it is some sort of crime."

"Why would they keep it from us?"

"I'm not sure I'm following you. Why are you making this into such a grand problem?"

"I'm not. I just don't know why they would keep it a secret. I've known Chester my whole life and the Reverend at least sixteen years now. You would think they would've told us that they were family."

"It's not as if they don't like each other Amalie. Maybe they just assumed that you already knew."

"Well, that's possible I guess. But it still doesn't explain why this portrait is haunting me. The face looks so familiar."

Erik took a closer look at the portrait and then turned to his wife. "It does seem familiar. However, I can't place it either." He scratched his head and then cupped his chin with his hand. "It's strange….yes, but not criminal. I don't know what to tell you my love. I'm sure it will come to you and if it doesn't it shouldn't really matter should it?"

"I suppose not. However, this glimpse into their family's history has made me think about your family."

Erik's eyebrows went up. "My family?"

"Yes, I would like to know more about your family. You've never really spoken about them at all."

"Why should I? They were only present for a short time in my life and the time they were present they rarely had any contact with me at all. It's not as if they loved me. They only tolerated me until they could figure out another way to deal with me."

"Even so I would still like to know more about them. After all, they helped to shape the person you are."

"You mean the person I *was*. The person I am now had nothing to do with them."

"You may not think so but they did. Everything that they did or didn't do still influences you......even now."

"Perhaps. Actually, even though my mother was a callous and sad woman she did allow her servant's daughter to sit with me.....to teach me. She was the only friend I ever had when I was a small boy. I called her "M". I remember not being able to say her name so she told me that I should call her "M". She was a young girl of sixteen and I was almost four years old. She taught me to read, write and more importantly she taught me about music. Her father had been a pianist but had developed a condition which took the use of his hands from him. To keep the music alive he taught his daughter to play, she in turn taught me to read music. I wasn't allowed to go near the piano that was in the house but on days that my mother would go out, which was very seldom, "M" would sneak me into the great room and allow me to play. I memorized each note and its sound so that I could play the music in my head."

"She sounded like a wonderful friend. I'm surprised she wasn't afraid of your appearance."

"From the day I met her, she never once showed any prejudice against me. I did wear my mask most of the time when she was around but there were a few times when I wasn't afraid to go without it. Of course, when my mother saw me without it, she would scream in horror and make me immediately put it back over my face. I'll never forget the fear in her eyes or the shriek of her screams. It seemed that my face stole her soul from the minute she laid eyes upon it. As for "M", she saw my face many times and never gasped or cowered in fear of what she saw. I wasn't sure why she had such a kind soul but I know now that God had sent her to protect me and teach me so that I could survive on my own. I hadn't thought of her in years. I wonder whatever became of that beautiful soul."

"Do you remember her full name Erik?"

"No, I only know that her initials were M. O. M. It's rather ironic that her initials spell out the word mom. She was definitely more of a mother to me than my own mother was at any point in my life."

"What about your father Erik?"

"What about him? He was rarely home and when he was he never once spoke to me or even looked in on me. It was as if I didn't even exist. I think he wished secretly that I didn't."

"I don't know how anyone couldn't love their own child. I don't care what they looked like." Amalie said shaking her head and then joined Erik on the edge of the bed. She grabbed his hand and then put her head on his shoulder.

"I'm sorry that I brought up such a painful subject for you."

"It's quite alright. The past doesn't hurt me. It only reminds me of who I never want to be again. Is there anything else you would like to know about my family?"

"No, but I would like to know why you left? You had "M" there to protect you, so why did you need to leave?"

"My dear friend "M" had grown up. She had just turned twenty and would soon be leaving to serve another family in the city. We lived far away from the village so that no one would ever see me. We were well hidden from the eyes of speculation and ridicule. "M's" mother wanted her to go work in the city where the wages were increasing for women in her occupation. Also, my mother was soon to have her second child and I had overhead them planning to put me in an institution. I knew that I didn't belong there so after my sister was born I left......never to return and never to be sought after. I knew that they wouldn't come looking for me. They were probably relieved that the monster had disappeared."

"Did "M" not worry for you or look for you?"

"I'm sure she did but she also knew that if I didn't want to be found that she nor anyone else would ever find me."

"Do you know where your sister is?"

"No, and please don't try to find her Amalie. She had nothing to do with what happened to me. She is innocent in all of it and I wish to leave her that way. I just pray that my mother and father were able to give her what they couldn't bring themselves to give me; love."

"I love you Erik Geraurd." She leaned over and kissed him passionately on the lips.

"What was that for my dear?"

"Not being bitter and angry."

"Why should I be? My life has turned out well. After all I have the most beautiful wife in all of France sleeping next to me every night and our precious child who gives me so much joy that I sometimes think it is all a dream."

"Yes, you do and don't you forget it." She kissed him again and then laughed.

"I don't think you will let me," he laughed.

They gave each other a tender embrace and sat quietly for a moment. Amalie's curiosity about his sister was definitely peaked but she would honor her husband's wishes.....at least for now. It was almost certain that his sister was probably never told of his existence but then again, whispers and rumor usually find their way to the people that aren't supposed to know. He was right to want to leave her as an innocent party to his tragic tale. She was insignificant and it would only raise more questions about him which would put his life under a magnifying glass. No, his sister would remain anonymous; keeping the secrets he held buried.

"I suppose I should get some rest before I begin preparing supper."

"Didn't you know that the girls were already taking care of that?"

"No, I didn't. Why are they preparing the meal so early?"

"It's not early my dear. I think you are losing track of time more quickly these days. It's nearing six in the evening."

"I guess my preoccupation with this portrait has deprived me of the hours. I'll go help the girls. I'm sure they could use another set of hands."

"I'm sure they would welcome your company. I know that Louisa wanted to show you how grown up she is becoming."

"Yes, this trip has definitely given her the opportunity to explore many new things. However, I will be happy to return home and back to our daily routine."

"And I too look forward to that day. Do you happen to know when that will be Amalie?"

"I believe we should be able to return home in four days. Claire should be well enough to care for herself by then."

"Then I should start preparing for our return. I'll go to Remy's tomorrow and see what he may need my help with before we depart. I'll also have to go into town tell the coachman to prepare for our eminent departure. Is there anything you require me to get for you while I'm there?"

"No, I believe I have all that I need. If I find that I do I'll let you know."

She exited the room, leaving him standing in the doorway. He watched her walk down the hall and into the kitchen. He didn't want to alarm Amalie but he too was interested in why the portrait on the wall looked so familiar. He walked across the room and took another look at it. It was evident to him who the portrait reminded him of and if his suspicions were correct then Chester would have a lot to explain. It would appear that Chester had just as many secrets to keep quiet as he once had.

# Farewell

The time came for them to return to Trie-Chateau. While Erik helped the coachman load their luggage onto the coach Amalie and Louisa said their good-byes. Louisa gave Odette a tender embrace as the tears streaked down her cheek. "I'm going to miss having you to talk to every day."

"I'm going to miss you too, Louisa but I promise that I'll write to you every week. And when Mother is able to travel once more we will come for a visit."

A smile erased the frown that had been on Louisa's face. "Did you hear that Mother? They will come to visit soon."

"Yes, I heard my child. I look forward to their coming."

Claire hugged Louisa and then Amalie. "Thank you for everything you have done for us. I am so grateful that you came. Please give my cousin Henry our love and could you please give him this for me?" She handed Amalie the portrait that had been hanging above the bed where they had been sleeping.

"Yes, I'll be happy to give it to him," Amalie said.

"Tell him that it's my way of thanking him for sending you to us. This portrait belongs with someone who is directly related to Jean Troudeaux. I don't think he's ever seen it."

"I'm sure it will be received with the same love in which it was given."

Remy shook Erik's hand and then gave him a fatherly embrace. "Thank you for all of your help and I wish you a safe journey home."

"Thank you Remy. I hope to be seeing you soon. I am glad that I have such an honorable man to add to the list of friends I have made in my life."

"And I am honored to say the same."

Erik shook his hand one more time and then helped his wife and daughter into the coach. Louisa pressed her hand against the glass window of the coach while the tears continued to stream down her face.

Odette walked over to the coach and pressed her hand against the glass, mirroring Louisa's.

"I'll never forget you," Louisa said.

"Nor I you," replied Odette.

Her hand slipped down the glass as the coach slowly moved away from her. Somehow Louisa knew that it wouldn't be the last time she would see her friend but even so she would miss her until she saw her again.

It was late when they returned from Etrepagny. The house was quiet and the air in the house was chilled. The stale smell of the house being closed up for two weeks wafted above them like a thick fog. They were happy to be home. The exhaustion in her daughter's steps was duly noted by her mother. So, Amalie picked her up and carried her to the top of the stairs and into her room where she laid her on her bed. After helping her change into her night clothes, she tucked her into bed, kissing her on the forehead and whispering good night. Erik with the aid of the coachman unloaded the luggage from the coach. After thanking the young man for his help, Erik made his way to the back of the house to retrieve some wood so that he could build a fire in the fireplace. The air was much colder than it usually was during the early autumn months. As he gathered the firewood he noticed a flickering light near the stable. He dismissed it at first believing it to only be the flickering of a lightning bug but then the flashes became more brilliant.

He dropped the wood and ran into the house. He barreled into the study, fumbling through the drawers of the desk. Amalie saw him as he raced to the study and met him in the doorway as he made his way to exit. "Where are you going with that?" she asked as she pointed to the revolver that was in his hand.

"I'm going to the stable."

"Is there trouble Erik?"

"I don't know, but there is definitely something or someone out there."

"How do you mean?"

"I'll explain later, Amalie. Stay upstairs with Louisa and watch out the window. If anything happens take Louisa into the cave and stay there."

"Shouldn't you get Chester or Peter to go with you?"

"There's no time. I'll be all right."

He kissed her on the cheek and then exited the house through the front instead of the back so that he wouldn't alert whoever it was that he was aware of their presence. He made his way down the gravel road that led to Peter's house and then made a quick entrance into the trees so that he could approach the stable without being seen. As he came upon the stable, he could see no lights and no signs of anyone. The horses were calm and silent.

Erik quietly opened the stable door, peering in to see if he could see anything. The moon had slipped behind some clouds which gave him cover from being seen if there was in fact, anyone to see him. He entered and then closed the door behind him. He walked slowly from one stall to the next hoping he wouldn't be greeted by an angry assailant. He reached the end of the stalls without any incident and was relieved. He wanted to be sure that there hadn't been anyone there so he decided to light the lantern to have a better look. As he reached out his hand to retrieve the lantern, a hand came out of the shadows and grabbed his. Erik pulled his revolver, pointing it into the darkness. A low voice shouted frantically, "Don't shoot Erik. Don't shoot. It's me, Hessam."

Erik pulled the man closer so that he could see his face in the moonlight. It was indeed his friend. "Good heavens, man are you trying to get yourself killed?"

"Of course I'm not; quite the opposite actually."

"What are you doing here? Better yet, why couldn't you just come to the house?"

"I went to the house but no one was there. We, Darius and I, remembered the cave and so we've been hiding there until you returned."

"And just whom are you hiding from Hessam?"

"The Shah's men are convinced that I or you have something that belongs to them and although I think they believe they killed me, I don't think they'll give up looking."

"So you came here knowing with full knowledge that you would put my family in jeopardy."

"I came to get your help. I wanted to warn you so that you wouldn't be caught off guard. And don't be so self-righteous, if you hadn't stolen what they are looking for to begin with we wouldn't be in the situation we are in now."

"And what is it that you are referring to Persian?"

"You know quite well what I am referring too."

"Ah yes, the Red Diamond. The trinket that you gave to my wife without telling me you had done so."

Hessam could see the disappointment in his eyes and hear the discontent in his voice.

"Yes, and you gave it to me without telling me that it was a stolen gem of the utmost importance. Your treachery against the Shah won't go unpunished Erik. They will not rest until they get it back."

"Yes, but I am thought to be dead so why would they come looking for me?"

"They didn't come looking for you, they came looking for me and in doing so they revealed that they knew of our friendship and that you had survived. I told them of how you lived in the Paris Opera House cellars and I even convinced them that you must have hidden it there although you were dead now. That is when they made me take them to see it for themselves. I was able to make it appear that I had drowned while trying to raise the gate for them but I don't think they will give up that easily."

"I see. You do have a situation which requires some thought and planning."

"Couldn't you just give it back to them Erik? I assume that Amalie is still in possession of it?"

"Let's just say that its whereabouts are known to those that need to know of it at this time."

"Whatever do you mean?"

"I mean that if you don't know you won't have to answer for it. So, don't ask me its whereabouts again. Now tell me, where were these men the last time you saw them?"

"They were wringing their clothes out after being unsuccessful. Then I overheard them say that they were going to go back to my flat to search for the diamond. They believed that I may have been untruthful in my account of its whereabouts."

Erik scratched his head and then put his arm around his old friend. "I want you to go back to the cave to get some rest. I'll come in the morning and we'll discuss this further. I'm afraid if I don't get back to the house soon Amalie will become worried and then I will have to involve more people than I care to in this."

"Erik, I'm sorry for all of the trouble but I didn't know where else to go."

"It's fine Persian. It's not as if this was the first time we had to get out of an impossible situation. It's unfortunate that they made the discovery but hopefully we'll be able to come up with a solution."

He patted his friend on the back and opened the stable door. Hessam began walking toward the clearing where the cave was located. His dark skin glistened as the moonlight hit his face. It reminded Erik of the night they parted ways all of those years ago by the shore. They were both much younger then and more aware of what their adversaries were likely to do with them. He never thought the day would ever come that his secret would have been made known but then again there were many things that had happened to Erik that he never thought would ever happen. One of them was waiting for him at the place he called home. He made sure that the stable door was shut and then made his way back to the house where his anxious wife greeted him with a loving embrace and a kiss on the cheek.

"I'm so glad that you're back. Is everything in order? Was there anyone to find?" Amalie spoke quickly flinging her questions at him like a knife thrower would fling his daggers at his target….one after the other.

"Yes, everything is in order. However, my old friend Hessam seems to have found yet another way to bring excitement into my life."

Amalie drew back and gave him a puzzled look. "Hessam? What does he have to do with what you found at the stable?"

"*He* was *who* I *found* at the stable. It seems that he is no longer able to stay at his flat due to an unexpected discovery by his previous employers."

Erik saw that the look on his adoring wife's face was a clear indication that it was time for him to reveal to her all that transpired before he had ever made his way to Paris. He walked her into the great room and seated her on the sofa. He then took her hands in his and told the story of the night that he stole the Red Diamond of Nadirijna. When he finished his tale she sat stoically staring into the unlit fireplace.

"Why, Erik?"

"I did it for Hessam. I knew that he would never take it if I told him that it was the Red Diamond. He's under the assumption that it is of a greater value to the Shah than it is to anyone else. What he doesn't know or even understand is that it is rightfully his."

"I'm sorry Erik but I'm not quite sure how a stolen gem can be rightfully anyone's except the original owner."

"You're right Amalie. That is why Hessam is the rightful owner."

"Is this some kind of game you are playing with me? If it is, it's not much fun."

"No my love, it's not a game. Hessam is the rightful owner of the Red Diamond or at least his ancestors are. You see Hessam is only half Persian. His mother was a descendent of India. She was the great granddaughter of Ganrila the Emperor of India. You see in the mid-18th century when the Shah Nadirijna invaded India, the Emperor had nothing in the government treasury to offer as retribution to the Shah so he gave him the Red Diamond and a few other precious jewels from his personal safe. Nadirijna wasn't satisfied with only these few items and so the Emperor was forced to give him two of his daughters, Apsara and Dulari. Nadirijna brought them back to his palace and made them his servants. The Empress Apsara he took as his mistress and fathered a child through her. Hessam's grandfather was that child. After Nadirijna was assassinated, both women were murdered and the child was given to a Persian woman to rear as her own child. This was done with the hope that any trace of the indiscretion of their former Shah would be erased or at least silenced. They also had kept the child in order to be able to use him as leverage if they found themselves at the mercy of the Emperor of India. A bargaining chip as it would seem.

Hessam's grandfather was just a small boy then and was told nothing about who he truly was but his mother had given him a ring before they drug her off to her death. His grandfather didn't know it but it was a ring that only the royal family of the Ganrila Emperor was allowed to wear. Hessam only showed it to me once in a moment between friends that were sharing their heartbreaks. Hessam's grandfather was unaware of his royal heritage as is Hessam. To them the ring was just a reminder of someone they had lost. He only knew that his mother's family had been enslaved and made to do things against their will and then put to death when they were of no use. He was ashamed of whom he had become and also ashamed that there wasn't anything he could do to change it. He felt as if he had betrayed his true family his entire life, especially since he was so involved in upholding the very things he knew had caused such pain to his own mother and grandfather."

"What a terrible story Erik. And how do you even know that any of it is true?"

"In my travels to India I met many people and they were willing to share their tales of the battles and outcomes of them. They were all very similar in detail. Only a few of them denied the two empresses being taken or enslaved but the Red Diamond was always mentioned. That was the main reason I agreed to work for the Shah. I wanted to see this famed Red Diamond for myself. It was only later that I learned that Hessam was the great grandchild of the once enslaved empress."

"How is it that you know he is an heir but he doesn't?"

"Because he was never told of the royal ancestry from either side of his family in order to keep him from rising up and perhaps making a claim to the throne of Persia or rebelling and avenging the throne of his ancestors from India. Instead they kept a powerful hand on anyone that was born from that lineage, keeping them close enough to control but also close enough to use for their own purposes. He was only told that his great grandmother was not Persian and that she had been taken from her family and had been made to be a servant of the Shah."

"You still haven't answered my question. How do you know?"

"The walls of a palace tend to whisper and when you are a part of the walls many things are heard. Sympathizers are found everywhere and in my old life I was quite capable of getting people to tell me what I wanted to know. Let's just leave it at that."

"Just because someone told you, doesn't make it true."

"Perhaps. However, the ring that Hessam owns is the only proof I need. The fact that his account about the events is so closely related with those that live in a region so far away is all the proof I need."

"Stories are carried all around the world Erik. What difference does that make?"

"Because a true Persian would never defame the name of any Shah no matter what he had done, that's why. The loyalty that Hessam carried for his employer was merely out of duty and survival. Hessam, like me, struggled deeply with who he was because of a past he had no control over. I guess that's why we became such good friends."

Amalie leaned toward him and kissed him gently on the lips and then caressed his cheek with her hand. "I'm glad that you're his friend Erik. And I am certain that together you'll figure out a way to solve this problem. However, I don't think keeping the gem is the answer. No one is going to ever believe that Hessam is an heir of the Emperor of India."

"Hessam is royalty in many ways but you're right. No one would believe it and I honestly believe that Hessam hasn't made the connection between the diamond and his past. I think he merely sees the wrath of the Shah's men directed at him because of what was taken. He obviously never knew the importance of it when I gave it to him or he would've never given it to you."

"Or perhaps he did and he just didn't care about it. It was a very long time ago Erik. Sometimes it's just best to leave the dead where they belong....buried."

"Nevertheless, it's a situation which requires my attention and the sooner the better. I certainly hope that these men didn't find a way to follow them here."

"Them? Darius is with Hessam?"

"Yes and they have been staying in the cave while they waited for our return."

"I see."

"I'll make sure that they find other accommodations away from here as soon as we devise a way out of these circumstances."

"That won't be necessary. They can stay in the guest room. I think it is best that we keep a close eye on them. No one would ever think to look here and we can always move them back to the cave if there is any evidence of trouble." She began walking toward the staircase and then turned to speak. "It's unfortunate that an act that was meant to return honor and pride back to your friend has now come back to create chaos and mayhem. Sometimes honor and pride will make honorable men look foolish when they aren't willing to give it up."

Erik's eyes glared at her as she quickly turned to go up the stairs. He knew that she was right. It was his pride that had talked him into stealing the precious gem from the Shah. He had wanted to show the Shah that he was smarter than he was and by stealing the diamond out from under his nose would prove it. At the time it seemed to be the right thing to do. After all Hessam was his friend and would soon be risking everything to free him from death so why shouldn't he be properly rewarded. Now that he was wiser he knew that the only reward Hessam needed was simply seeing him live. He should've just left it at that. Now his actions had brought misfortune upon his friends and could possibly bring it to his own family. Regret was usually not something that he entertained but tonight it seemed to be the emotion that consumed him.

Erik went to the study, took a seat at the desk and opened his Bible. He read for more than hour and then decided to turn in for the evening. The words of his mentor, Gaston, came to mind as he walked up the stairs. "Remember, you are only a man and men need God's help for all things….big or small." This was definitely one of those times when God would need to rescue him from his previous follies. It was never a thought in Erik's mind that his past actions would at this present time cause him to reflect upon other things he had done earlier in his life. He had thought that his past would stay where he had left it…..behind him. Now he knew that he would have to face and deal with the consequences of his choices. Regrettably, so would his friends and his family.

Details

*T*he morning brought the warmth of the sun as it shone through the cracks of the drapes in Louisa's room. Amalie was already up tending to the days chores and making breakfast while Erik stood at the foot of his daughter's bed watching her sleep. He walked over to the drapes, pulling them tightly to hide the sun. His precious child was exhausted from traveling and he decided that she should sleep a little longer this morning.

As he exited her room, he began thinking about what would be the best way to go about handling the situation that had been brought to his attention by his friend Hessam. It would be something that would have to be handled delicately as he knew as well as Hessam that the Shah of Persia was not a man that would be willing to concede defeat. However, there was something about Hessam's story that puzzled him. Why would the Shah send two men to persuade the Persian to give up the gem? Why wouldn't he just have him arrested and taken back to Persia? Something about the two men's story didn't add up. He wasn't sure but he definitely didn't believe these two men were ever sent by the Shah. He would have to find out just who they were before he could proceed.

"Good morning," Amalie said as she greeted him with a kiss on the cheek.

"Good morning, my love. Breakfast smells delicious."

"Where is our little angel this morning?"

Erik pulled a chair out to seat her at the table and then seated himself. "She's sleeping. I couldn't bring myself to wake her. She looked so peaceful and it was evident that she was tired from our journey back from Etrepagny."

"We shall let her sleep for a while longer but she will need to rise soon or her food will get cold."

"I'm sure she'll be up soon. The aroma of the meal you have cooked will certainly entice her."

Just then Louisa bounded into the room, fully dressed with her hair uncombed. "Good morning Mother and Father. I'm so glad that you made crepes and bacon. I'm so hungry."

She struggled to get the heavy chair away from the table so that she could sit to eat. Erik rose from his seat and helped her move the chair so that she was perfectly positioned to reach her plate and all that was on it. They continued to eat as they talked about what they would be doing the rest of the day. Erik made no inclinations as to his plans to investigate all that his friend had told him, instead he told them that he would be going to visit Peter and check on the business. Amalie was planning to continue the chores of the day and enlist her daughter's help in order to do so. They finished dining and Louisa removed the dishes from the table while her mother began washing them.

"Father, I hope you don't plan to be gone all day. I still need to practice using the magic powder."

"I'm sorry my child but your lessons will have to wait for another day. I have pressing business to attend to today and tomorrow. However, your mother needs your help today and I know she will be very happy to have you helping."

"But chores aren't fun like playing with the magic powder."

"I know Louisa but sometimes we have to do things that aren't a lot of fun but are necessary. I would rather be here with you but I have been away from my business for so long that I need to be there today. Your mother needs your help and if you help your mother then perhaps she will have time to do something fun with you today."

"All right Father. I'll help Mother. I'm very good at hanging out the clothes. Mother has told me this many times. I don't think she would know what to do if I didn't help her."

"Very well then Louisa. Go help your Mother and I will be back before supper."

He kissed her and then hugged her tightly. "I love you."

"I love you too, Father."

She skipped out of the room and into the kitchen.

He gathered his things and then before exiting the house Amalie met him at the door. "Promise me that whatever you and Hessam decide to do about your situation that you will include me in your plans?"

"You say that like you don't think I would."

"It's not that I don't think you wouldn't, it's just that I don't want to be the last to know." She smiled at him as she straightened his tie.

"You'll be the first one to know, I promise. Now I must be getting on or I'll not have time to go see Hessam and Darius before I go to Peter's."

He kissed her on the cheek and then said, "Don't worry, everything will work out. I'll be home in time for supper."

He exited the house through the front door and made his way out to the stable. He saddled Jasper and rode out to the cave. When he entered the main room, he found Hessam sitting on the small sofa reading a book.

"Well, my friend, I see that you have found something to pass the time. Where is Darius?"

"He is asleep in the bedroom. We are taking shifts sleeping just in case the two men that were after us happen to have figured out where we are."

"It's very unlikely that anyone would find you here but I understand your concern. Hessam, I'm going to get right to the point of my visit this morning. There was something about your story that has puzzled me. Are you absolutely sure that these two men are employed by the Shah?"

"No, I'm not. It's strange that you asked me that because I had wondered that myself."

"And what was it about them that made you wonder that?"

"It wasn't one thing actually, it was many things. For instance, their attire was representative of the Persian guard but they weren't quite up to the specifications that I remember. Also, they knew me by my birth name and not anyone that I knew, other than my family, was privy to such information. These men didn't seem to be too concerned about the Shah either."

"I suspect that they are imposters of the Royal Persian Guard and they are using whatever information they have been able to gather about you, me and the diamond to find out where it is." Erik scratched his head, rose from where he had been seated and began pacing around the room. "What I can't figure out is how they knew it was missing. They had to have some way of finding out that the jewel in the box was not a diamond but how?"

"Well, is it possible that they found your tunnel into the palace, and followed it until they reached the door that led into the treasury room?"

"It's possible but not likely. No one will ever find my tunnel entrance and if they did, they wouldn't be able to figure out where the latch to the door was to release it." In that moment Erik realized that he had never spoken to anyone about the tunnel and the hidden door until recently. "How did you know about the tunnel and the door, Hessam?"

"Ah, so it is true. You did contrive a tunnel that the Shah was unaware of then."

"Again, Hessam, how do you know about it?"

"The two men told me about it."

"Well, then I guess it is possible that they found it. However, they lied about the Shah not knowing about the door. He knew it was there. In fact that is why he ordered me and all of the other workers to be killed as soon as it was completed. Our knowledge of this particular tunnel was dangerous and my being able to open the door was even more of a threat to him."

"Why did he have it built?"

"He wanted to be able to escape the palace along with his many treasures without anyone seeing him if he were ever attacked by a foreign power."

"That makes the identity of these two men even more questionable."

"Is it possible that they were a couple of the workers that had been ordered to their deaths but somehow escaped?" Erik asked.

"It's not likely but then again, neither was your survival and yet here you stand in front of me."

"Yes, Persian and I have you to thank for that."

"Yes and I have you to thank for this mess that we're in now." He chuckled as he rose to fill his cup with more tea.

"You won't get an argument from me. I take full responsibility for what has happened. However, it is because of who you are that I risked so much to give you what was rightfully yours."

Hessam looked at him with a puzzled face. He didn't understand what Erik was telling him. "How do you mean?"

Erik proceeded to recant the same story that he had told to Amalie the night before and when he was finished the Persian sat almost catatonic on the sofa. He was in disbelief and shock.

"Hessam, are you all right? I didn't mean to surprise you with such a revelation into your past but I believe at your age it is time that you knew the truth about why your life was spared after they found that you had let me go. It wasn't because of your long service; it was because of your ancestry. You are a prince of Persia and an heir to the Emperor of India. They couldn't very well kill one of their own. Of course, it didn't hurt that they also thought I was dead but it was your heritage that kept you receiving funds from the treasury and breathing air."

He couldn't believe it. It was too much for him to process.

"How do you know that this is true Erik?"

"Oh, I'm glad that you can still speak. I was beginning to worry about you."

"This is no time for folly Erik. How do you know that it's true?"

Erik walked over to Hessam and grabbed his hand. Pointing to the ring on his pinky finger he said, "This is how I know it's true."

"It's only my great grandmother's ring."

"Maybe to you it is but to the former Emperor of India it was a gift to his daughter, the Empress, on her fourteenth birthday. It's a royal ring that only those who are of royal blood are allowed to wear."

"Again, how do you know these things?"

"I have traveled the continents of the east and met many people who confirmed that the markings on your ring are those of the royal family."

"So what am I supposed to do with this knowledge?"

"Nothing if you wish or you may take the Red Diamond with you and return it to your family where it belongs. Perhaps with this gesture they will see that you are who I know you to be."

"And who is that exactly?"

"You are a prince among the most common of men but not because you were born into it but because you have conducted yourself in this manner since the day I met you."

"What if I don't want to live my life as such? What if I like how I live now?"

"Then by all means, live your life the way you choose."

"Why would I only want to claim my throne to India? Why shouldn't I claim my rightful place in Persia?"

"Because the Persians don't see you as one of them or they would have made you Shah long before the current Shah was ever put in place. No, Hessam, you were only Persian when it suited them. Your life would only benefit from going back to India or staying where you are now."

"And where exactly is that Erik? I am running from two men that if they find me alive will try to kill me all over again and my home is no longer a safe place to live. I'm nowhere Erik; that is where I am." His anger at the situation was growing and it was evident to Erik that it was time to put his mind at ease about his safety.

"You're safe and you always will be as long as you stay here. Amalie has asked that you both come to the house for supper tonight. You'll enter through the secret door in the study. She has made up the guest room for you both. One of you will have to sleep on the floor but I think you'll find it more accommodating than the cave. Her only request is that you stay out of sight of the windows so that if anyone who is not welcome is lurking around they will not be alerted to your presence."

"Your wife has always done more than what is asked of her. She is a gift that is to be treasured. I'll be sure to thank her at supper." A smile appeared on his face as he spoke about Amalie's kindness. "However, you still have yet to tell me how we are going to rid ourselves of these two men."

"Patience, Daroga, Patience. It is always best to proceed with caution especially when you don't know your enemy. I believe we'll have to draw these men out into the open so that we may find out just who they are."

"And just how do you perceive to do that?"

"I have to go meet with Peter and then after I have spoken to him I'll let you know."

"What does Peter have to do with any of this?"

Erik put on his cloak and began walking toward the exit. He turned to his friend and said, "He has contacts in Persia that will be most helpful to us," and then he entered the tunnel that led out of the cave, closing the door behind him.

Another Face

*E*rik arrived at Peter's and Isabel's chateau just as Peter was exiting through the front door.

"Good morning Peter," Erik shouted to him.

Peter walked up to Erik as he got off of his horse. After his feet were firmly planted on the ground he grabbed him and gave him a brotherly hug.

"It's good to see you my friend. I would like to be able to say that you weren't missed but as you know it would be impossible for me not to miss you. It would be like trying to not miss my right arm if it had been cut off." Peter hugged him once more and as he pulled back he kept his hands on his arms. "It is so good to see you. I didn't expect you to be back to work until tomorrow."

"Yes and that was my plan also but it seems that I am in need of your help about a different matter," Erik told him as he straightened his waistcoat.

"You have my attention. What is it?"

"Not out here. Let's go inside."

"But Erik, I have a client that is meeting me at the office this morning."

"Does it look as if it could be a lucrative deal for us?"

"It won't make us rich overnight but it will definitely keep our families fed and roof over our heads."

"Then go and I will meet you there in two hours."

"Why not go with me now?"

"You know I don't like the negotiations when it comes to our business dealings. You're the businessman. I'm the creator. I'll be here in the drafting room finishing the plans for the addition to *your* house. I won't be late, I promise."

"Suit yourself. Let yourself in. The door is open. Announce yourself though. I wouldn't want Isabel to think you were a burglar. She's become quite skilled in shooting her pistol."

"Thanks for the warning!" Erik shouted as his friend rode away on his horse.

Erik turned his horse over to one of the stable boys and then entered the house.

"Now what did you forget Peter?" said a delicate voice.

"Peter didn't forget anything but I have forgotten how much I missed your voice."

As soon as she recognized his voice she walked quickly to the door. When she saw him she flung her arms around him. "Oh Erik, it is so good to see. How are Amalie and Louisa? How was your trip?"

"It's good to see you too, Isabel. The girls are fine and the trip was well.....interesting but I will let Amalie fill you in all of the details."

"Are they at the chateau?"

"Yes and I'm sure that they would be glad to see you and the girls."

"We're going to go visit them just as soon as I can get the girls ready. What brings you here anyway?"

"Do I need a reason to come see my favorite neighbors?"

"No, of course you don't. However, Peter isn't here. He's gone to the office."

"I know. I ran into him on my way in. But if it is all right with you I'm going to stay for an hour or so to work on the plans for the addition."

"That'll be fine. Just be sure to lock up before you leave. I wouldn't want anyone surprising me like you just did,' she laughed, 'although, it was a wonderful surprise. I'm so glad that all of you are home." She kissed him on the cheek and hugged him again before she left the room.

Erik removed his coat and hung it in the foyer closet. He then entered the study where he found the drafting table just as he had left it. It was good to know that some things never changed. Peter was a wonderful friend, actually one of the best friends anyone could ever have but no one would ever accuse him of being organized. His filing system consisted of five stacks of papers that he kept on his desk and when he ran out of room, he would move it to Erik's drafting table. He was pleased to see that no stacks had been added to those that had already been placed there before he left. It was going to be a challenge but he would need to find a place to put the stacks of papers so that he could continue his drafting of the drawings for the house. He looked around the room and found a small table next to the window that held a few small framed portraits on it. If he cleared it off, he could stack the papers there.

Erik picked up the frames from the table and placed them on the chair. He then moved the two stacks of papers to the table. Then he picked up the frames and placed them on the mantel of the fireplace.

As he set the second one down the man's face in the picture caught his attention. It looked very familiar but he didn't know why. He walked quickly out of the study and into the foyer and began calling for Isabel.

Isabel came down the stairs and met him in the foyer. "Yes Erik, what is it?"

He handed her the picture and asked, "Who is the man in this picture?"

She took it from him and studied it. "It's my father."

"Are you certain?"

"I know it's faded but I know what my father looks like," she laughed. "Why?"

"He looks like someone else I have seen in another picture. For some reason I can't remember where."

"Who does it look like?" Isabel inquired.

"That's just it, I'm not certain. In fact, I'm not even sure of where I saw the face he looks like. If I didn't know any better I would think my mind is playing tricks on me. It's not possible for me to have seen two different men's faces that remind me of one, is it?"

"Oh, so now there are two faces. Erik I would say that your journey was long and you need to rest."

"Don't be absurd Isabel. I'm all right. The portrait at Madame Brun's house was almost identical to the one of your father which I guess is not all that strange being that your father is the nephew of their cousin."

"Which cousin is that?"

"Surely you jest? You must know that Reverend Troudeaux is your father's uncle?"

The surprise on her face was visibly acknowledged by Erik. "You didn't know?"

"No, he's never mentioned having an uncle that lived close to us."

He held his chin in his hand; rubbing it as he pondered the information he had just been told.

"That's very strange indeed. I wonder why he never told you. However, knowing Chester like I do, nothing seems to surprise me. He has always been a bit eccentric and quiet when it came to matters of a personal nature."

"Well, eccentric or not, I'm rather offended that my father has kept this information from me my entire life."

"Promise me Isabel that you won't ask him."

"Why? Don't you want to know his reasons for not telling any of us?"

"I do, but I believe that sometimes a man's secrets are better left hidden until he is ready to reveal them himself. Remember, I'm a man that had many secrets and until I was ready to tell them, it didn't benefit anyone to try to reveal them for me. No, your father will definitely tell you someday soon."

"How can you be so certain?"

"He will have some explaining to do once Amalie gives the picture of your great grandfather to the Reverend. It's a gift from his cousin's daughter-in-law. Remember that he is also just as much to blame as your father in this exclusion of information. I think they will both have a lot of explaining to do."

"I suppose you're right. How can either of them keep it a secret once they find out that you already know?"

"And I have my suspicions that he wanted us to find out or good ole Uncle Henry wouldn't have sent us there. He had to have assumed that there was the possibility that we would come to this knowledge on our own."

"Do you truly believe that Erik? That they wanted you and Amalie to find out?"

"Anything is possible but of course, it is never good to assume anything."

"All right then Erik. I will let it go for now but if you find out anything will you please let me know?"

"Of course I will. It would be like trying to keep something from my wife…..impossible and absolutely not profitable if I tried."

"Very well then, I will see you later. The girls should be ready now. Don't forget to lock up when you leave."

"I won't."

Erik returned to the study with the frame held firmly in his hand. The similarities of the pictures were astonishing but it wasn't the picture that Madame Brun had given to them that haunted his mind. There was a picture that was in their chateau that it reminded him of but it was impossible to believe that it could mean anything. For now this mystery would have to go unsolved. He had more pressing matters to attend to with the situation surrounding his old friend. He set the frame on the mantel and then returned to his drafting table where he began drawing the plans for the new room that was to be added to his colleague's chateau.

Assistance Needed

*E*rik arrived at the office about a half hour after the new clients had left. Peter was sitting behind his desk working on finalizing the contract when Erik came through the door.

"I was beginning to wonder if you were actually coming."

"I was delayed by an unforeseen conversation I had with Isabel this morning."

"And what may I ask was it about?"

"It's not important and I'm almost certain she will tell you the details when you return home."

"Is this your way of telling me that it's none of my business?" Peter chuckled.

"No, it is just my way of saving you from having to hear the same story twice. Besides, it's truly not anything worth repeating twice. Still, the matter that I spoke to you about earlier is quite pressing and in need of our attention."

Erik sat in the chair that was placed in front of Peter's desk, moving it closer so that he could speak without raising his voice. He didn't want anyone to overhear what he was about to tell Peter. It wasn't likely that anyone would hear them but he never assumed anything. He told Peter the story about the Red Diamond of Nadirijna and then he told him of Hessam's past and about the current situation that had arisen. Peter, as usual, was not surprised at any of the stories he was told. After all, he and Erik had been friends for almost seven years and he knew of his questionable past. The day that he had learned of Erik's life beneath the Opera House was a day that solidified their friendship even more. Peter, even then, didn't judge him. He actually shared in his pain and anguish; understanding that his life was not representative of how anyone should ever have to live. No, Peter was as any good friend should be, ready to help and eager to jump into the fire without worrying about getting burned.

"So, how does this situation that you're in involve me?"

"I'm glad you asked that question. It is your involvement that will be the most crucial and helpful. I need you to contact one of your business associates in Persia and obtain some information for me."

"Let me guess. You would like me to find out if there is to be any reconstruction done on the palace and if so we would like a chance to make a bid on the job?"

"That would be quite helpful but what I truly need to know is if the Red Diamond is believed to actually be missing and if the Shah knows anything about it."

"Why does it matter if the Shah knows?" Peter asked as he pushed his chair back from the desk and made his way to the edge of the desk where he perched himself.

Erik answered, "If he knows that it's missing then it's possible that the two men aren't lying about why they are searching for the red diamond. However, if neither he nor anyone else knows then these two men aren't who they say they are and obviously are out to take something that was never theirs to retrieve."

"This is a delicate situation in which I won't be able to reveal much information. If I do then the Royal House of Persia will suspect that I may possibly be trying to lessen their load of treasures," Peter deduced.

"That is why I have called upon you Peter. You are the slyest of men and the most charming also. You could talk a cat out of its fur."

"Your flattery is noted and accepted. I do have a flare for the verbal extraction of others secrets. I consider it a gift."

"Yes, and I consider it a gift that will hopefully keep Hessam from parting with his head as well as me from mine."

Erik stood and walked over to the cabinet where they kept the brandy and glasses. This occasion called for some refreshment. He poured a glass for Peter and then another for himself. They drank as they worked out the details of the letter he would send to his contacts in Persia. It was a perfectly worded letter and hopefully they would have answers in a month or two. Until then, Hessam and Darius would remain in their home as guests where he could make sure they would stay out of trouble. They continued to work until late afternoon and then they locked up the office, returning to their homes.

The Truth

The rest of the week was uneventful and then it was once again Sunday morning. Erik was glad to be back at the piano in the church playing the hymns that he had grown so fond of the past six years. As the Reverend Troudeaux closed the service with a prayer, Erik anxiously waited for him to finish so that he could invite him to dinner. The Reverend made his way to the entrance of the church so that he could speak with his congregation as they left. Erik cleared the music sheets from their stands and covered the piano keys with the cover. He hoped that no one would invite him for dinner before he was able to do so. He looked for his family and saw that they had already exited the church. He approached Reverend Troudeaux and extended his hand for him to shake. The Reverend reciprocated and shook his hand.

"Thank you for the wonderful message this morning Reverend."

"You're welcome Erik and thank you for the beautiful music. There's nothing like heavenly sounds to soothe the soul and fill your heart with joy."

"I agree. Reverend will you be able to join us for dinner today?"

"Well, I believe I *am* joining you for dinner. Your lovely wife has been gracious enough to ask me to come dine with you and I accepted immediately. No one makes stew as good as your wife."

"No doubt, she makes a wonderful stew but it seems that she has read my mind today as well. Then we shall see you at the chateau shortly?"

"Yes, I have a few things I need to tend to before I come but I will be there soon."

Erik met Amalie, Louisa, Meg and Chester at the coach as they were boarding. Chester was no longer able to drive the coach or to tend the horses. The last six years had taken its toll on him and his age was becoming evident in every movement that he made. Amalie had relieved him from his daily chores four years ago, as well as Meg but kept them employed as overseers of the new coachman, Luc and house servant, Yvette, a young married couple they had hired to take their places. The routine for Yvette was the same as it had been for Meg; only coming on Mondays to clean and help do chores. Luc's duties were also as Chester's were while he was the coachman; tending to the horses in the morning, cleaning the stalls and preparing the coach as it was needed. A condition of their employment was that they were to live in the small cottage with Chester and Meg. This was Erik's way of making sure that Meg and Chester had the help they needed as they grew older. At first Luc and Yvette weren't fond of the idea but once they became more acquainted with them they were glad that they lived there.

Yvette and Luc were atop the coach waiting for the last person to board. Once everyone was inside they left the church and made their way home. Sunday dinner was a tradition at the Geraurd chateau. Everyone, including Yvette, Luc, Hessam and Darius took part in sharing the meal and giving thanks for all in which they had been blessed. The Reverend arrived shortly after they had finished setting the table and the food was being brought to the table. Everyone came to the table, Erik blessed the food and they ate. After the meal was finished Erik and the Reverend Troudeaux retired to the great room while the women cleared the table and washed the dishes. Hessam and Darius returned to their room to continue the game of chess that they had begun earlier. Yvette, Luc, Chester and Meg excused themselves from the after dinner rituals so that they could return to their cottage to rest.

Erik and the Reverend exchanged light conversation while they sat in front of the fireplace. Amalie walked into the room carrying the frame that held the old charcoal drawing that Madame Brun had given to her. She sat next to the Reverend and handed it to him.

"What is this, my dear?" he said inquisitively.

"It's a gift from Madame Brun. She asked me to give it to you. She said it was a gift to thank you for sending me to help her."

He took it from her hand and then stared at the portrait. It brought back many memories; some good and some bad. His eyes swelled with tears and his voice cracked as he spoke; trying to choke back his emotions.

"I haven't seen a likeness of my grandfather in many years. He looked as fierce as a lion but in reality he was as gentle as a lamb."

"Why didn't you tell us that you were Chester's uncle? You had to know that when you sent us to help Claire that it was a possibility that we would find out."

"Yes, Amalie, I knew that it was a possibility and if I am to be completely honest I actually prayed that you would find out."

Erik and Amalie glanced at one another with bewilderment in their eyes.

"Why?" Erik asked.

"Erik, I've grown tired of living in silence about my relationship to Chester and what I have kept secret for so many years."

"And what exactly have you kept secret Reverend Troudeaux?" asked Amalie.

In that moment it became clear to Erik whom the man in the portrait shared a resemblance. "May I have the portrait for a moment sir?" he asked the Reverend.

He handed it to him and then Erik excused himself as he walked from the great room into the drawing room. Amalie and Reverend Troudeaux followed him. When they entered the room, Erik was comparing the portrait to a painting on the wall. Amalie moved closer, however the Reverend didn't. It was as if he already knew what was about to be revealed. Erik's face had lost all of its color as he stood staring in disbelief at what was in front of him. Amalie gasped at how closely they resembled one another. He turned to her and asked, "Had you ever seen the man in this portrait before you painted this portrait of me without my disfigurement?"

"No, Erik. The first time I ever saw it was while we were staying in Claire's home. I reconstructed your disfigured face based on what you looked like."

"Then I believe the Reverend has some questions to answer."

They turned to question him and he was no longer in the room.

"Where is he?" Erik asked.

"I don't know."

They walked into the great room searching for him but he wasn't there. Then they searched the study, the sitting room and still didn't find him. Finally, they entered the dining room and found him sitting at the table with his head buried in his hands, weeping.

"Reverend, forgive me for not showing much compassion in this circumstance but I believe you have a lot to explain." He took the framed portrait and put on the table in front of the Reverend. "Why is it that my face resembles a man that I have never met?"

"I can't answer that for you. It isn't my story to tell."

Erik's voice became more agitated and his anger could visibly been seen on his face.

"Then whose story is it?"

A voice from outside the door replied, "It's mine."

Chester entered the room and put his hand on his uncle's shoulder. "It has been a long time that I have asked you to stay silent Uncle and it was wrong for me to burden you with my secret for all of these years.

It's time that Erik hears the truth not from you or anyone else but from me."

"My silence isn't what makes me weep, it is the joy that will come from the silence being broken that makes these tears come forth."

"I'm not sure that Erik will find the joy in it as much as you and I but I pray that he will."

"Would the two of you please stop conversing like I'm not in the room? What is supposed to bring me such joy?"

At that moment Meg, Isabel, Peter and the girls, Bella and Nicole entered the room.

"We're sorry to barge in on you but we went out to the cottage to visit with Mother and Father but they weren't there when we arrived," Isabel said apologetically. "Yvette told us that they were on their way here. Apparently Father forgot his cane."

Peter observed that the mood of the room was not one of a joyous Sunday celebration but more of a funeral. He detected the discontent on Erik's face.

"Is everyone all right? Did someone die?" Peter asked with a bit of levity in his voice.

Chester turned to his son-in-law and spoke, "No Peter, no one has died. Everyone will be all right as soon as I'm able to tell them what I have wanted to tell them for the past six years." He put his hand on Erik's shoulder and motioned for him to have a seat. He then motioned for Amalie, Isabel, Meg and Peter to take a seat around the table as well.

"Amalie, where is Louisa?" Chester inquired.

"She's upstairs in her room."

"May the girls join her?"

"Why of course they may. She'll be glad to have company this afternoon."

Isabel stood up from her seat and kissed the girls on the forehead. "Go to Louisa's room and play now. We'll be up later to tell you when it's time to go."

The girls happily left the room and quickly ascended up the stairs to Louisa's room. Isabel returned to her seat at the table and waited patiently to hear what her father had to say.

Chester remained standing as he positioned himself between Meg and his Uncle Henry. "What I'm about to tell all of you will be difficult to hear but I believe that confession is good for the soul. I also hope that you'll all find it in your hearts to forgive me some day for keeping this from you for as long as I have."

Chester cleared his throat and began his story. "First of all, I'm sure you're all wondering how it's at all possible that the Reverend could be my uncle being that we are so close in age. You see, my grandmother gave birth to Uncle Henry only two years before I was born. It was a miracle that she was able to conceive at the age of forty but it was an even greater miracle that she survived giving birth."

Erik was growing impatient and interjected, "That's very fascinating but that doesn't answer my question."

"Be patient Erik, you'll have your answer in due time. Something so important can't be rushed."

Erik's demeanor changed quickly to that of a child being disciplined. "I'm sorry Chester, please continue."

"Many years ago when I was a young man working for Gaston's family, Gaston and I became very good friends. It never mattered to him that I was three years older than he nor did it bother him that we weren't in the same social class. I really didn't have to tell any of you that since you all knew him. It would be more of a surprise if I told you the opposite. Anyhow, I tell you this because it will become relevant later." He stopped for a moment to organize his thoughts and then continued. "Long ago, when I was a young man, I fell in love with a young woman who was married. I didn't know she was married at the time I met her. She was very beautiful and she found me to be charming. She was the first woman who ever paid the slightest bit of attention to me being that my social status was one of a common man. She was a flame and I was a moth that flew around her warmth. Regrettably the physical attraction between us clouded all of my senses and caused me to make decisions that would change my life and those who knew me forever. It was six months that we had been together and then one night she came to me and told me that she was with child. This was when I found out that she was married but she didn't love him. Her marriage had been arranged by her parents in order to keep their vast estate and wealth within the upper social classes; ensuring their lineage would survive any financial disasters. She explained that she knew that the child could only be mine because she hadn't been with her husband in months. Then she informed me that she couldn't continue to see me. Her husband was already beginning to suspect that she may have been unfaithful and if she didn't return to him in that manner then there would be no need for speculation."

Amalie looked at Erik's face as the story was being told. She could see that his words weren't at all what he had expected to hear. She reached for his hand that was on top of the table and held it, squeezing it just enough to let him know that she was there. He raised her hand to his lips and kissed it, letting her know that her presence was a comfort.

"What happened to the child?" Isabel asked.

"Well, a few months after she told me about the expected child, she and her husband moved away. I didn't know where they had gone and I was devastated. I would never see my child."

"What did you do?" Peter inquired.

"There was nothing that I could do. I was miserable and I had no one to turn to in my time of need. Since I had been with a married woman it was unconscionable to tell anyone about our affair; not for my sake but for hers. I suffered alone and in silence for months until I received a letter from her. She told me that the baby had died during childbirth and it was best that it had."

"I'm so sorry Chester," Amalie said.

He smiled at her and replied, "So was I. It devastated me until one day about eight years later I met a woman by the name of Margaret Odette Morel." He grabbed Meg's hand and smiled. Erik's face became flushed at the mention of the name. He knew that name.

"Margaret Morel. That's what her name was Amalie," he whispered.

"Whose name?" she whispered.

"The young girl I called "M" when I was a boy," he answered her quietly.

Chester continued with his story. "Margaret was twenty years old and the daughter of a woman who was the housekeeper to a very wealthy family that lived near Rouen. After overhearing the mistress of the house tell her secrets to the priest that visited the house on occasion, she sought me out."

"Who was the mistress of the house?" Isabel asked.

"She was the woman that had broken my heart all those years ago. Mademoiselle Morel informed me that she had overheard her tell the priest that her son was not her husband's child. She told him that I was the child's father but she had told me that he had died. She was compelled to free her soul from the burden of the secret she kept because she felt that God had punished her for her infidelity by giving her a son whose face was not that of an angel but that of the devil."

Erik knew at that moment what Chester's secret was. The man that had ignored him for all of those years was just that; a man that meant nothing to him and vice versa. It had become clear who his true father was; it was Chester. It all made sense now. The past became more explainable and even more understandable with this small amount of information. Erik rose from the table and walked out of the room. Amalie rose to follow him and Chester motioned to her not to go. Instead he followed him into the great room where he found him staring into the fire.

"Erik, I'm sorry that I didn't tell you sooner. Meg and I wanted to tell you but we weren't sure how you would react."

"So why tell me now?"

"My reasons are those of a selfish old man that needed to know if his son would forgive him for not being there for him. By your reaction I'm sensing there isn't much hope that you will. I want you to know that we searched everywhere for you and only after a year had passed did we ever give up the search."

"Why did you bother at all? Didn't Margaret tell you how hideous my face was?"

"Erik, Meg told me all of the wonderful things about you, especially how gifted you were in music and yes, she told me about your disfigured face too. I saw you through her eyes and it didn't matter."

"Meg told you? How would she have known?"

"Meg is the name that I gave to her after we married. Margaret Odette Morel is my wife."

"How is that possible?"

"After Meg found me and told me her story about you and how you had run away, we looked for you for many months. We traveled all over Europe looking for you. We regretted that we were never able to locate you. As we traveled together we became friends and eventually I won her heart as she did mine. It was easy to love her since she loved you so much. Neither of us ever thought it would be so hard to find someone that fit your description but apparently you truly didn't want to be found."

"What would you have done if you *had* found me?"

"I would have loved you and taken care of you. You're my son Erik and no matter what your face looked or looks like I'll always love you. I loved you the moment Collete told me she was carrying you in her womb."

Chester's words weren't those of a man who had any regrets about his actions in the past but of a man who felt blessed to have found what he had thought was gone forever. He walked up behind Erik and put his hand on his shoulder.

"I hope that someday you'll be able to forgive me. I know I wasn't there for you when you needed me the most but…."

Erik turned to face him and interrupted him. "You're right, you weren't there for me when I needed you but you're not to blame. You didn't even know that I was alive. Which in turn makes me wonder how you knew that I was your son?"

By this time, the Reverend, Amalie, Meg, Isabel and Peter had joined them in the great room; quietly entering the room and seat-ing themselves so as not to disrupt the conversation between Erik and Chester. Chester turned to them and said, "This is something you'll all want to hear. Amalie's grandfather was a generous man when it came to many things. Gaston was too. He provided me with my own room in the stables. Which doesn't sound like much but for a man with very little means it was as grand as a palace to me. One night, about a month before I met Meg, Gaston and I had been drinking in the stable and swapping secrets. I had a little bit too much ale and I inadvertently told him about my love affair with the young woman and what had been produced from this lapse in judgment. Since I was always poking fun and making light of all things big and small, he didn't take me seriously. He thought that I was trying to make a fool of him until he met Meg and I asked her to tell him what she had witnessed. Gaston felt terrible that he hadn't believed me and he vowed that he would always keep a watchful eye and an attentive ear out for my son. Gaston gave me the funds that I required in order to search for Erik. He never once asked me to repay any of the money but then again, I never expected him too. That was just the way he was.

When it came that many years had passed and neither of us had ever found or heard about anyone fitting your description we assumed that there wasn't much hope that you had survived. Then many years later it happened that there was a need for Gaston to tell me his tale that was so unbelievable that I thought he had gone mad. He told me that he had met a young man by the name of Erik Geraurd that lived in the cellars of the Paris Opera House. He described your disfigurement, your talents and your intellect. That is when I knew that you had to be my son."

"Why didn't he tell you before then?" Erik asked.

"Gaston had seen how devastated I was when I had lost you the first time. He didn't want to see me go through losing you a second time if he wasn't sure that you were truly my son. It worked out that before he died he had been working on arrangements to bring you safely to the house. He had wanted to bring you here to give you a new life. It was unfortunate that he couldn't carry out his own plans but once he revealed to me everything he knew and had learned I was happy to help, even if it turned out that you weren't my son. Just knowing that I was helping someone that had possibly been through what my own child had been through was enough reason to trust Gaston's plans."

Erik's eyes filled with tears and Chester walked over to him. "I've been the happiest I have ever been for the past six years because you have been here with us. My family was completed the day you arrived at this house. I love you....... son."

Erik put his arms around Chester and hugged him. He was overcome with emotion and the words he wished to speak wouldn't pass through his lips. He released his embrace and looked Chester in the eyes. "I'm glad that it was you. I longed to have a father that would look at me, not ashamed and embarrassed, but with love and pride. Ever since I met you, you have done all of these things. You said earlier that you hadn't been there for me when I needed you the most but you were wrong. You were here to encourage and support me as I struggled with becoming a better man. You're here now and that's what is important. It is obvious to me now that God was always watching over me, helping me find my way home." Erik put his arms around him once more and embraced him. He removed his arms from around him and then walked over to Meg. He held her hands in his, looking into her eyes.

"God sent me many people to help me during my dark times. Meg, you were the first. I should have recognized you by your kind eyes. After all these years your eyes are just as bright and full of hope as the day I last saw you. I don't know how to thank you for all of your love and care when I was young."

"You already have. You're every bit the man I knew you could be if given the opportunity to do so."

"Is that why you agreed to help carry out Gaston's plans?"

"Yes, and in my heart I knew that it was you of whom he was speaking. No one tamed the black and white keys of a piano like you did. My only regret is having left you so that I could go to work in the city. I should've stayed to protect you."

"You couldn't have protected me. You were a young woman that had your entire life in front of you. In all of my travels I have learned one lesson that has stayed with me."

"What is that?"

"It's that we all choose the lives we have. I would've chosen to leave my mother's house whether you were there or not. It was that choice that saved me from years in a mental institution and put me on a path that although may have not been ideal, did serve me well. Certainly, the life of a gypsy may not seem appealing to some but for a child that had been locked away from the world for so many years, it was a new beginning and a world of possibilities. I learned many of my talents as I traveled in the carnivals. I don't regret that choice because it led me to the next person that helped me find my way home."

"And who might that have been?" a voice from above them asked.

Everyone looked up and saw Hessam and Darius standing on the staircase.

"Hessam, Darius come join us." They came to the bottom of the staircase where Erik waited for them.

"Have you been listening the entire time?" he asked Hessam.

"If I said no, would you believe me?"

"Of course not." Erik laughed. "Then I suppose you have heard the news."

"Yes, apparently you have a very good friend that helped you through the most troubling of times. I can only assume you were speaking of me."

"Hessam, it was you I was speaking of but I was referring to the news that Chester is my father."

"Chester is your father. Oh yes, I seem to remember that coming up in conversation earlier. It's quite remarkable but not surprising."

"How do you mean Hessam?"

"The first time I met him I thought that you had a striking resemblance to him. I thought it was only a coincidence but now it makes perfect sense."

"Hessam I think you like to make me feel as if I don't know anything. I don't believe one word of your nonsense. Nevertheless, he is my father and you are one of my dearest friends. Although at this moment I truly can't tell you why," he said jokingly.

Everyone in the room began to laugh and the solemn, uncertain mood that had been in the room changed quickly to one of laughter and joy. Amalie's face was damp from the tears that had rolled down her cheeks. Erik kissed her on the cheek and smiled. Then he walked over to Isabel and Peter. He took Isabel by the hand and kissed it softly.

"I'm sure this is as shocking for you to hear as it is for me but I want you to know how honored I am to have you as my sister. No man alive is as happy as I am at this moment to be part of such a wonderful family."

"Yes Erik, it's a lot to think about and please forgive me for my lack of enthusiasm. It's not that I don't love you or don't want to have you in my life as a brother, it's just not what I expected to hear," Isabel said with a dazed look in her eyes.

"I understand. Take all of the time you need," he said as he squeezed her hand.

"Peter, I hope this won't change our friendship," he said as he put his hand on Peter's shoulder.

"Why would it? I've always thought of you as my brother-in-law. Nothing could ever change our friendship, at least not for the worse," he said with levity in his voice.

"I appreciate that Peter."

Amalie joined them as they spoke. She put her arm around Isabel and led her to the sofa.

"Are you going to be all right?"

"Yes, Amalie, I'll be all right. It's just that I don't understand how Father could have kept this from us for so long. Everyone makes a bad decision here and there. We all know that. Did he think we wouldn't understand?"

"I don't know Isabel. That's something you're going to have to ask him."

Chester overheard his daughter's concerns and tried to put them to rest. "My dearest daughter it wasn't that I didn't trust you, it was Frederic that I didn't trust."

She looked at her father and he could see the question in her eyes. "You see there were many things that I knew about your brother Frederic that you didn't. What your mother and I knew about him was something we thought was best kept between the two of us."

"What could be so terrible?"

"Erik, Peter, please join us for a moment. Would the two of you mind going into the drawing room?" he asked Darius and Hessam. "I would like a moment alone with my family."

Hessam spoke first. "Of course, we will sir." He motioned for Darius to follow him and they entered into the drawing room and closed the doors behind them. Chester walked with the aid of his cane around the room gathering his thoughts while everyone waited for him to speak. There was so much that he needed to tell them but figuring out where to start presented his dilemma. The anticipation in the room grew as they waited. Each person thinking their own thoughts about what he was about to tell them. Tired from pacing, he slowly lowered himself to the hearth of the fireplace.

"First of all I want to make it clear that I loved Frederic very much. He was my son. Second, I want you all to know that this was the reason I had to allow what happened to him to take place."

There were gasps and glances exchanged after his brief statement then he continued. "The evening that Erik first met Frederic was a night that I shall never forget. I seem to remember Erik telling me that he thought someone had entered the house that night without being invited. He later found that it was only Sampson, the barn cat who had crept into the house. Well, that wasn't the truth which we all found out after he showed Amalie the letter he had taken from the study that had been penned in Erik's handwriting. Unfortunately, I knew it wasn't the cat when Erik first told me because I knew that it wasn't the first night that Frederic had broken into the Girault home.

Before your mother died, Amalie, he had stolen a letter that Gaston had written to my Uncle Henry explaining his discovery of a man that could possibly be my son. He wrote to him asking for his assistance in helping relocate him to a better situation. In the letter he described the physical conditions and challenges that the man faced so that he would understand the reason his help was needed. He thought that Henry's position in the church would be useful in creating a new life for him. I didn't know anything about Erik at that time. He asked Uncle Henry not to tell me anything until he was certain that this man was my son. Gaston didn't want me to know because he thought that if it wasn't him I would be devastated once again. Anyhow, with Frederic being privy to the information, you can understand how angry it made him."

Erik now understood why Reverend Troudeaux never questioned him much about his past when he had first met him. He had already known about him and what he had been through. The pieces of the puzzle seemed to be fitting and completing the picture that had once been as empty and unrecognizable as his face once had been. "How did you find out that he had the letter and that he knew about Erik?" Amalie asked.

"Do you really need to ask that question? You know how Frederic was. If he had information that he could use to manipulate you, he was going to use it to his advantage and would not hesitate to reveal it. It was after your mother's accident that he told me that he knew about my past and that he planned to tell his mother. Obviously it crushed him when he found out that Meg already knew. Then he threatened to tell Isabel and I assured him that her knowledge of such information would serve him no purpose either. He thought better of it and I assume never told her."

Isabel rose from where she had been seated and spoke softly. "Father, he did tell me but I never believed a word that he said. I told him that he had you confused with someone else and that it was an absurd accusation. Even after he showed me the letter I just assumed it was written about someone else's child. Your name was never mentioned and the letter never referred to Reverend Troudeaux as your uncle. I just found that out a few days ago myself. I never believed the story could be true."

"Then why are you so surprised now?" Peter asked her.

"I'm not surprised Peter. I'm ashamed that I didn't believe my brother. All he wanted was for me to believe him."

"But for what purpose did he want you to believe him? Was it not so that he could plot Erik's demise or to ridicule him? Frederic's motives were driven only by his selfish and arrogant ways. He would have used you to do his bidding and then turned on you just like he did his own wife." Peter said while touching Isabel's face with his hand.

"What you say is true but perhaps if we had given Frederic the opportunity to change then he wouldn't be dead now."

Chester stood up and walked to his daughter. He turned her to where he could see her face and looked into her eyes. "Do you not think that I gave him those opportunities? With all of the things that he had done by the time Erik arrived here, can you honestly stand there and say that we as a family didn't show him the same compassion and understanding that we gave to Erik?"

"You did Father. All of us did. But that still doesn't explain why he hated Erik so much when he had never known him."

"Actually it does. The day he told me that he knew about the monster that I called my son, he also told me that he would never accept him as family and that if I did ever find him he would make sure that he knew his place. I told him that the child had died at birth and that it wasn't possible that the letter was about him. It didn't seem to matter what I told him, he was determined to believe what he wanted to believe. It was evident that he was hurt because I didn't tell him about my past but I didn't think that it was important. It was the past and I couldn't do anything to change what had happened. I had hoped that he had forgiven me for not telling him but our relationship was never the same after that." Isabel reached for her father's hand and after grasping it in hers she kissed it. She could tell that losing Frederic still hurt him. He squeezed her hand gently and then turned to take a seat next to Meg on the sofa.

"When I told Gaston what Frederic had told me, he was forthcoming with what he knew of a man living in the cellars of the Paris Opera House. He never told Uncle Henry where the man lived or even his name, just that he needed help finding him a place to live. When he told me Erik's full name, I knew that it was possible that it could be him. I wanted Gaston to bring him to me immediately but with Frederic knowing what he did, Gaston thought it best to wait. It was unforeseeable that Gaston would get sick and not recover before he was able to send for him. I am grateful that Amalie agreed to carry out her father's dying wish to help Erik because in doing so she allowed me the opportunity to finally meet my son."

"I can understand waiting but why wait three years after Gaston's death to bring him here?" Isabel asked.

"I wasn't ready to take on someone else at the house after Father died. When he died it had only been three years that Mother had passed. I needed time to adjust and make sure that I could handle such an enormous responsibility," Amalie replied. "I was glad that my uncle allowed me to spend so much time in his flat in Paris. It gave me the opportunities I needed to learn more about who I was without my parents."

"Did Frederic ever speak to you about it again?" Peter interrupted aiming his question at Chester.

"He only mentioned it a few times after our initial conversation. Then days, weeks and months passed and nothing else was ever mentioned. Frederic had become more preoccupied with his law practice in the months following. He had broken his engagement to Amalie and then married Anna the next year. I thought that he had forgotten about everything until the night that Amalie introduced Erik to him. That was when I realized that whether he knew exactly who Erik was or not, he would stop at nothing to discredit him or harm him if the opportunity arose. That's why after Erik and Amalie married I went to Erik and told him that he needed to do whatever he had to in order to protect his family. Frederic was so jealous that Amalie had chosen someone who looked like Erik to be her husband. I think he always loved you, Amalie. I'll never understand why he broke off the engagement."

Erik and Amalie exchanged glances. They knew why he had to do it but they would never tell anyone what they knew about him murdering her mother all those years ago. It was best that the shame of his actions stay buried with him. Amalie held Erik's hand tightly as she listened to him speak. She couldn't help but remember that terrible afternoon when Frederic had come to the house determined to kill her or anyone in his path. The thought of it sent a chill up her spine.

"That not only explains why he hated Erik so much but it also explains why he didn't want his own wife to have a child. It's evident that he thought it would be born with a disfigured face too." Amalie said, with her voice lowered and filled with sadness.

"Yes Amalie, your observations are correct," Chester replied. "He feared that if he had a child it would be less than perfect which he thought would somehow reflect upon him. It's sad that he wasted so much of his life trying to manipulate the world to fit how he believed it should be instead of just accepting the wonderful gifts that God gave him no matter how they were presented."

"It sounds like Frederic was a lot like my mother," Erik interjected. "Except she thought God was punishing her for having relations outside of her marriage. She believed that I was her punishment for her sins. I would have lived the rest of my life believing it was true if it hadn't been for Gaston. God has blessed me time and time again even when I didn't deserve it. I took the people and things that happened in my life for granted not realizing that it was all part of a plan for God to bring me back to my family. It would seem that no matter what I did to change the plans, He always found a way to bring it to fruition." He leaned over and kissed Amalie on the cheek. "I finally understand what Gaston meant when he said that I needed to wait on the Lord and not do things in my own powers."

The Reverend Troudeaux interrupted Erik saying, "When we act in haste and do not wait upon the Lord we may delay his plans but we never change them as long as we come back to Him and seek his guidance."

"Well said, Reverend," Peter proclaimed. "Now if we are done emptying all of the skeletons out of the family closet, I would like to propose that we have some tea and dessert in the drawing room."

Isabel smiled at him and then kissed him on the cheek. "I for one am glad the skeletons are gone. I have gained a brother, a sister-in-law and a niece all in one day. I can't think of a better day than this one."

"Then I shall get the tea and dessert," Amalie chimed in cheerfully.

"I'll help," replied Isabel and Meg simultaneously.

Erik opened the drawing room doors and they joined Darius and Hessam who were in the middle of a game of Euchre. Erik immediately went to the piano and began playing one of his favorite songs that had a lively tempo which represented what he was feeling. It was as if someone had placed him inside his childhood dream; the one in which he was loved by his parents. Although he knew his mother would never be able to utter those words to him, he was glad that his real father had. If he had met his father before now he would probably have been more angry about why he hadn't tried harder to find him but being a father himself made it easier to understand that nothing Chester ever did in his life was ever easy. He could see it in Chester's eyes that every day that he didn't know where he was, was a day that a little bit more of his heart died. A slow torture that was invisible to everyone around him. He knew his pain all too well which he suffered at the hands of his own mother.

In the years after he had come to live with Amalie he realized that it wasn't that his mother disliked him so much, it was herself that she despised. It was her own actions that led to her circumstances and rather than accepting responsibility for them it was easier for her to hate and blame him for the direction her life had taken. He too had made some bad decisions in his life in which he had blamed others. It was Gaston who had made him see that no matter what others had done to him, he was still responsible for his own actions.

He had hated his mother for years but now he pitied her for not knowing how good her life could have been had she just been honest with herself and those around her. He didn't like to think much about her but when he did he would try to remember the goodness that she had in heart for allowing "M" to be his friend. It was because of that friendship that he had been reunited with his father. Remembering this one thing made forgiving her for all the other things she had done much easier. As he played, the room filled with stories of the past and plans for the future. He knew once more that God had blessed him, not with just the physical presence of a family but with the knowledge that his family truly loved him and wanted him.

Sleuth

S everal weeks had passed since Peter had sent the letter to his contacts in Persia. Erik knew that it could possibly be months before
they heard anything but was growing impatient. His house guests had
been with him for nearly two months now and they were still no closer
to solving the riddle of the two men who had presented themselves
as part of the Royal Guard from the palace of Persia. Peter was also
growing impatient waiting for news from the east. In fact, he was very
curious as to the whereabouts of the two men, being that he loved a
good mystery. So he took it upon himself to locate them.

He had planned a business trip into Paris earlier that week in which
he had led Erik and Isabel to believe that conducting business was the
sole purpose of going. However, while there he also began his own investigation into the whereabouts of the two men. What he found out
was quite shocking. Apparently the men had taken up residency in
Hessam's flat. Some of the local merchants informed Peter that they
had introduced themselves as Hessam's uncle and brother but had wondered why they hadn't seen Hessam or Darius. Peter didn't tell them
where Hessam currently was but put their minds at ease by going along
with the lie that they had been told; confirming that the men were the
relatives of their loyal patron. He did this so that they wouldn't uninten-
tionally alert the men that they knew something was awry. It was best
if the merchants continued to believe the two men's story. This would
make it easier for him to check on them. Peter told the merchants that
Hessam and Darius were on holiday and that the men were watching
over his flat until they returned. He had also spent an entire day watching to see who they spoke to and where they went. What he learned
from his surveillance was interesting. He knew that Erik would also
find it interesting.

When Peter returned to Trie-Chateau he was anxious to inform
Erik of all that he had learned about the men. He arrived at the office
just after Erik had locked the doors. Peter took his key to the office and
opened it, walking inside gesturing Erik to follow.

"I wasn't opening the door Peter, I was closing it. I'm on my way home."

"I think you will want to stay to hear what I've found out about our two imposters."

"And what is it that you've learned?"

Peter proceeded to tell him all that the merchants had told him. It was clear that Erik was relieved to at least know that they hadn't found out that Hessam had survived.

"Well, Peter it seems that you have out done yourself this time. How come you didn't tell me of your plans?"

"I didn't want you to worry about me. You've had enough to think about these past few weeks with all of the news about your father. Consider it a gift."

"I do consider it a gift; a very useful gift. Now that we know that they are staying in Paris we can possibly find out who they are and why they have decided to make Hessam's life so incredibly unbearable."

"I inquired as to why the two men said they were at Hessam's flat and the butcher shop owner told me that neither of the two men would say. He said they seemed reserved and quiet; trying not to be noticed."

"I'm sure they don't want to draw attention to themselves. That would only make more people ask questions as to who they are. Which again makes me suspect that they weren't sent by the Shah of Persia," Erik said while rubbing his chin.

"It's peculiar that you should mention that. While they sat at a café drinking their coffee I was able to overhear part of their conversation as I hid behind my morning newspaper. It seems that they have become quite taken with the Paris Opera House while they have been in the city. I observed them walking on the Rue Scribe many times in one day where they always asked the workmen about how soon the cellars would be relieved of the water. This incidentally made it easier to understand the conversation I overheard. It seems that they are planning to return to the lower levels of the Paris Opera House as soon as the water has been pumped out of it. Their speech suggested that they were looking for something and that they were certain it must be there. I didn't hear all of their conversation because of a waiter dropping a tray full of china but I can only guess that they were referring to your red diamond. The man with the scar under his eye was nervous like a mouse caged with a cat. He looked around often and prompted his friend to keep his voice lowered."

"Doesn't sound like the behavior of innocent men," Erik said while pouring Peter a glass of brandy. He poured a glass for himself and then sat behind his desk. "Did they mention anything about how long they would be staying in Paris?"

"No, there wasn't any mention of how long they would be there. However, the younger of the two said something about the secret they carried possibly costing them their lives if the Shah ever found them."

Erik took a drink of his brandy and then put his feet up on his desk, stretching his arms behind his head and then clasping them behind his neck; thinking about what Peter had just told him.

Peter asked, "Now why would the Shah want them dead if he was the one who had sent them after the Red Diamond?"

"I don't know Peter but I'm almost certain that you'll not rest until you find out."

"I could say the same thing about you, brother-in-law, since you're the reason I now have more instances to unravel mysteries and follow strangers in big cities. My life was not dull by any measure before I met you but knowing you has definitely caused my life to be less predictable."

"Believe me when I tell you that I wished it were more predictable and less eventful at my age. However, it was pointed out by my wife that all of this has transpired because of my own prideful ways and it is my responsibility to make it right. The worst part of that observation is that I agree with her."

"Well, Erik you're wise not to argue with Amalie about such things. If I have learned one thing about your wife it is that her wisdom is something that shouldn't be ignored. I believe that God bestowed that upon her at an early age."

"Yes, and she frequently bestows it upon me," he said as he rolled his eyes and laughed. Peter found the humor in his words and laughed with him. By this time Erik and Peter were gathering their things and making ready to leave. Peter slapped Erik on the back and said, "Well you should be grateful that she does. There's no telling how much trouble you would be in without her."

They walked to the door, opened it and then walked out of the office closing the door behind them. Peter locked the door and Erik stood waiting for him. "Yes, I imagine I would have died a horrible death by now if it hadn't been for Amalie. I owe her much if not all of my happiness."

"And don't you forget it Erik. There are few people in this world that are as wonderful as my Isabel and your Amalie. We're both lucky men to have such women find the good in us and want to live with us for the rest of their lives. If I were a woman I would've thought more than twice about marrying the likes of me but somehow Isabel needed less than five seconds to make that decision," he said as he laughed a hearty bellowing laugh.

"Well, we both better get home before they regret making their decisions," Erik laughed.

"I agree."

They mounted their horses as the cold wind swept across their faces. The sky was gray with only a few breaks in the clouds showing the sun for brief moments. As they began to ride off a young man who was yelling "Peter Durand" ran up alongside of him. Peter stopped and then Erik. The young man handed him an envelope with a postmark from Persia. Peter thanked him and tipped his hat.

Peter handed the letter to Erik. "I believe this is for you."

Erik looked at it and then without hesitation opened it. The wind was picking up and the paper was flapping violently in his hand. "I can't read it here. I'll have to read it when I get to the house. I want you to be there when I read it Peter. Can you come over after supper?"

"I don't see why not."

"Then I shall see you later this evening."

Erik tucked the letter into his inside coat pocket and they rode toward their homes.

Message Received

When Erik arrived at the house Louisa had just finished setting the table. Amalie placed the dishes for their meal out onto the table and they sat down to eat. Erik was unusually quiet as Louisa tried to engage him in conversation by telling him about what she did while he was at work. His responses were short and not as animated which made Amalie wonder what was on his mind.

After they finished eating, Erik excused himself from the table and Louisa and Amalie cleared the table. He went to the closet in the foyer and pulled on his coat. He then exited through the door in the kitchen to go retrieve a load of firewood to place into the fireplace in the great room. Amalie noticed him leave but didn't say anything to him. She thanked Louisa for her help and then sent her into the drawing room, instructing her to practice playing the piano. When Erik came to the back door with his load of firewood she met him at the door, opening it for him.

"Thank you my love."

"You're welcome." She closed the door behind him as he began to walk toward the great room. She followed him even though she hadn't yet finished cleaning the dishes from supper. As he put a log on the almost smoldering fire he could feel Amalie's stare on the back of his neck as she stood behind him.

"Is there something you need Amalie?"

"No, I was just wondering why you were so quiet at supper tonight. You seemed a bit preoccupied."

"You worry too much my dear. There's nothing preoccupying my mind except this." He turned to face her, put his arms around her waist, pulling her to him and kissed her passionately on the lips. He hadn't kissed her like that in a very long time. Their relationship was always full of passion but it seemed that the routine of daily life had taken its toll on how much time they actually spent together. She threw her arms around him and continued to kiss him. He hadn't realized how much he needed to feel her arms around him at that moment but when she began to pull away from his kiss he pulled her even closer to him, resting his chin on her soft brown hair.

"I love you Amalie."

"And I love you Erik. However, don't think that I've forgotten about your silence at supper. I know there is something preoccupying your thoughts and it isn't kissing me."

He pulled his chin away from her and looked into her eyes, still holding her in his arms.

"I should know better than to try to keep things from you. You're more effective at tracking a trail than a blood hound."

"So you have been keeping something from me."

"Yes but it wasn't intentional. I have received a letter from the east today but haven't had the opportunity to read it. I was going to tell you everything after I had read it."

"Why haven't you read it?"

"Well, since it was written to Peter, I wanted him to be present when I read it."

"Please tell me you haven't involved Peter in all of this."

"I could tell you that but it wouldn't be true. Don't worry Amalie, his involvement is minimal and only for gathering information which I couldn't obtain seeing as how I'm supposed to be dead."

Just then a knock was heard on the front door. Erik walked to the front door and opened it. Peter was standing outside. His appearance was that of a man who had come through a blustery wind; red cheeks and hair tossed.

"Come in before you catch your death," Amalie said as she greeted him with a kiss on the cheek. She took his coat and scarf from him and then hung them in the foyer closet.

"I'll let the two of you conduct your business while I return to my chores." She gave a crooked smile to Erik and kissed him on the cheek. "It's good to see you Peter and Erik don't keep him too late. I wouldn't want Isabel to worry about him."

"Why would Isabel worry about me? She already knows the company I am keeping," Peter laughed.

"That's reason enough now isn't it?" Amalie laughed as Erik and Peter laughed with her. She walked into the kitchen leaving them alone in the foyer.

"Shall we go into the study?"

"Yes, I think that's a good idea. I wouldn't want to Amalie to overhear anything that would raise her objections."

They opened the door to the study, entered and then closed the door behind them. Peter made his way to the cabinet where the brandy was kept and retrieved two glasses and the decanter. He placed them on the desk, opened the decanter and poured. He handed Erik one glass and kept the other.

Peter raised his glass in a gesture of gratitude and said, "This is just the thing to take the chill off an evening as cold as this one. I thank you and my cold bones thank you."

"You're welcome Peter but I think I'll save mine just in case this letter doesn't present the information we were hoping to receive."

He pulled the letter from his coat pocket, opened it and began reading it aloud.

> *Dear Monsieur Durand,*
>
> *I was surprised to receive a letter from you after all of these years but it has brought much joy to my heart to know that you are well. I am well also and my family has grown by two more children since we last spoke. I miss France dearly and hope to return soon. I know that you didn't write to me to hear about my personal life so I will get to your inquiries.*
>
> *In the matter of the Royal Palace moving the treasury to a new location I can confirm that this is true. The palace has grown to be a place where more and more foreign leaders come to visit and the Shah saw fit to have them moved to a more secure location. As for the safety of the movement of the treasures, everything has been accounted for, even the famed Red Diamond of Nadirijna. Although it was once thought to be a deadly gem at one time it seems that it is no longer true. It is now on display atop the Shah's head as a magnificent ornament adorning the center of his turban. I had thought that the Red Diamond of Nadirijna would never be worn again since the curse of it had all but been validated by the demise of every Shah that had dared place it upon them; meeting a terrible fate. However, it seems that we now have a Shah in which the curse no longer applies. This has made him more powerful and more intimidating to those who dwell outside and within the palace. So the answer to your question as to if the Red Diamond of Nadirijna will be able to be viewed is yes. However, you may only ever have that opportunity if you find yourself in the company of the Shah.*
>
> *As for the renovations that you spoke of for the palace I can't confirm that any are being done on the treasury*

room. Rumors are that the entire room has been locked up and the only person that holds the key is the Shah himself. No one seems to know the reasons behind it but now that the jewels and other treasures are no longer there, no one seems to bother about it.

I believe your last question concerned the head of the Royal Guard. I am assured that he is still at his post as are all of the others that serve there. Being that I am not a native of this land I am not trusted with a lot of information. However, I have obtained information on good authority from a Persian colleague of mine that there was an investigation into a situation that occurred almost six months ago. It seems that two of the Palace's Royal Guardsmen have gone missing and no one knows why or where they have gone too. Of course, all of this has been kept from the public and those that have knowledge of this situation fear telling anyone due to the fact that the Shah now seems to possess a power to ward off anything that might harm him. I for one don't believe there ever was a curse and that all of the incidents would have fallen upon the former Shahs no matter what jewel they had chosen to wear that day. I'm sorry that I could not have been of more assistance. If I find that there is any need for your services in the region I will contact you again. Give my best to Madame Durand and the children.

Sincerely,
Monsieur André Petit

Erik handed the letter to Peter and he skimmed over the words. Erik sat on the edge of the desk facing Peter who was seated. He took his glass of brandy and drank the entire contents. Peter poured another glass for both of them and then took a drink from his. Peter stood up and then walked around the chair where he had been seated and waited anxiously for his companion to speak. Erik was mulling over the contents of the letter, he then took it from Peter to review what he had read. The silence blanketed the room like a cloud of fog.

"I suppose this means that the two men could possibly be the ones that are missing and that they could have been sent by the Shah. However, it seems that the elusive gem isn't missing at all. At least the Shah doesn't seem to know it."

Peter began pacing the floor and then turned toward Erik. "Perhaps the Shah knows that the jewel he is wearing is not the original Red

Diamond of Nadirijna but he doesn't care. Look at the results he has gotten from donning his cursed jewel without a fatal incident occurring. It's made him powerful and intimidating."

"Yes, it would seem that it has worked to his advantage if he truly knows that it's not the real gem. I guess the monetary value of a rare gem would be outweighed by the political and social power the Shah has gained by the assumption that he could overcome such a curse that has claimed so many of his predecessors. However, if he doesn't know it, then why would these two men from his Royal Guard be looking for it?" Erik scratched his head and began walking around the room while sipping his brandy.

"The one man said that the secret they carried put their lives in danger if the Shah ever found them. I'm curious as to what the secret is." Peter took the letter from Erik's hand. "Do you think the Red Diamond is their secret or is it something else?"

Erik gave his companion a quick pat on the back and said, "Maybe the secret is just that; a secret. It seems that the room where the secret tunnel enters the palace is now locked up tightly and that no one knows a reason as to why. It's very odd behavior for my former employer. Why would he lock up a room that is empty? Especially since there are only four people left that have knowledge of the secret entrance into and out of the palace from that room and two of them are his missing guards."

"Odd behavior indeed. It's as if he suspects that someone else who poses a bigger threat knows about it. Is that what you are thinking, Erik?"

"Yes, my friend, it's exactly what I was thinking. Still I don't have the slightest clue who would know such a thing. Unless......"

Peter chimed in, "He believes that you may still be alive."

"Do you think that after all of these years he truly believes that I am still alive?" Erik asked as he took the letter from Peter's hand to gaze upon it one more time. He stared at it as if it would somehow give him the answers he so desperately needed.

"Anything is possible Erik. If he believed that a red diamond could cause him harm from just wearing it, then it is possible that he believes that you have risen from the dead. I for one am glad that you're not among *my* enemies. I don't think I would stand a chance against your cunning ways."

"I didn't know someone as charming as you had any enemies Peter and remember that the only reason I'm still alive was not because of my cunning ways but because of Hessam's. He was the mastermind behind my escape. It's regrettable that the others that he involved in helping me betrayed us when they were given the opportunity."

"Look at it this way Erik, at least those two men still believe that you are truly dead now. They'll never come looking for you. Now as for Hessam, it's hard to say what his fate will be. They obviously didn't believe that your dying once was enough so it's possible that they won't believe that he is deceased either."

"Your reasoning is fascinating Peter. I think sometimes that you must be related to my wife."

"I'll take that as a compliment and I won't tell Amalie that you were making light of her analytical skills again."

"It was meant as a compliment to you as well as Amalie. It's always good to have someone point out the obvious."

"Well, with that comment I think I'll return to my family. It's obvious that my presence is no longer needed here," he chuckled as he drank the last swallow of his brandy.

"I appreciate your help Peter and you know that for as long as I breathe air I'll need your assistance."

"Yes, Erik and when you decide what you plan to do about your situation I'll be there right behind you pushing you to the front as I cover the rear. I like to think of myself as a warrior but only if someone is in front of me."

"Sometimes bravery isn't measured by the action but by the intent. You're intentions are always meant for good Peter and I hope you're serious about helping me execute my plans."

Peter opened the door to the study, walked into the foyer and pulled his coat and scarf from the closet. He put it on and then as he flung his scarf around his neck he said, "I'm always serious when it comes to helping my family. You can count on me to be wherever you need me to be whenever you need me to be there."

Erik opened the front door and watched as Peter climbed atop his horse and rode out of sight. He was glad to have received the letter from Peter's longtime friend although instead of answering his questions it appeared to create more that needed to be answered. Why would the Shah secure a room in his palace when the only two people that knew about the secret entrance were he and the Shah? It didn't make any sense. Perhaps there were others that had gained knowledge of it and this was why he was taking precautions to make sure that no one would enter the palace through it. There were several scenarios that ran through his mind but he couldn't settle on one that truly painted a clear picture of whom the two men were and why they were looking for the red diamond that was obviously not missing. He would have to figure out a way to get the two men to tell him or someone exactly who they were and why they had risked so much to obtain a gem that was not missing.

As he shut the front door Amalie entered the room. "Louisa is waiting for you to tell her good night. She missed you listening to her practice. I told her that you and Uncle Peter had some urgent business to discuss. She's very understanding for a six year old."

"I'd say she's a lot like her mother." He kissed her on the cheek and then put his arm around her as they walked up the stairs. "I'll make it up to her, I promise."

"She's getting very good at playing but I think her heart lies with the magic you've been teaching her. She has a heart for adventure and things of wonder.....much like her father."

"That's what worries me," he laughed.

They reached Louisa's room and when they entered she was already asleep in her bed. Erik sat next to her, leaned over and kissed her forehead. "Goodnight my sweet child. May your dreams be of extraordinary adventures where you're the heroine." He kissed her one more time and then exited the room with Amalie.

As they walked to their bedroom Amalie inquired about his meeting with Peter. He informed her of what the letter said and also told her of what Peter had learned from his trip to Paris. She was glad to know that the two men were not where they could cause them any harm but she knew that it wouldn't be long before Erik decided that he needed to be in Paris too.

# Plans

The blustery winds from the north brought the colder air and a light frost which covered the ground. Erik rose early so that he could begin planning how to find out just what it was the two strangers knew about the Red Diamond of Nadirijna. His routine was to gather wood for the fireplaces and the stove in the kitchen, light them and see that they burned for a while. Then he would retire to his study to read his Bible until Amalie called for him to join Louisa and her for breakfast. He finished gathering enough wood for the fireplaces and returned to his study except this time when he entered he was not alone. Hessam sat in the high backed chair that sat in front of the desk with the letter that Peter's friend had written in his hand.

"Good morning Hessam," Erik cheerfully said as he walked to his chair behind the desk. "What brings you down here at such an early hour?"

"I overheard you and Peter in the foyer last night. I know I shouldn't have listened but it is my life that has been disrupted and I hope to get back to some kind of normalcy soon."

"It's quite alright Daroga. You're more than welcome to read the letter. I had every intensions of showing it to you today anyway. I was hoping maybe you could make some sense of what was written."

"Unfortunately Erik, I am just as lost as you are on this matter. I have no explanation as to why two men from the Royal Guard would be missing, why the Shah isn't worried about it or for his personal choice to lock a room in the palace that sits empty. However, I'll tell you what I do know for certain and that is that the Shah knows that the gem he is wearing is not the Red Diamond of Nadirijna."

"How can you be so certain, Hessam?"

"Because there isn't a shah alive that would wear that jewel unless he knew otherwise. Besides, you and Peter aren't the only ones that have friends in Persia."

"Ah, my dear friend, you have been up to your old sleuthing ways once again. I knew that somehow you would find a way to get to the bottom of this. So, what is it that you've discovered?"

"My sources don't know that it isn't the real Red Diamond but they claim that the Shah sent out one of his best royal guards to search for the other lost one. However, his orders weren't to bring him back if he was found. He was to be put to death."

"Did he have any idea why he was sentenced to die?"

"You know as well as I do that it must have something to do with the Red Diamond. Nevertheless, it appears that the Shah had accused him of being a traitor. Therefore, the man sent to find him was to kill him."

"And why would a royal guard be so important? What could he possibly know?"

"I couldn't tell you but it's obvious that the lost guard knew too much no matter what it was he knew."

"So did he find the man?"

"No. The guard that was sent never returned. It has been rumored that the two men are dead; both fatally wounding each other. Of course, neither you nor I believe that is true."

"So tell me Hessam, what is your theory on what happened to the men?"

"I believe they are both still alive and that they're living in my flat awaiting the day that they can make their way into the Paris Opera House cellars to look for the jewel which they believe you hid there."

Erik stood from where he was seated and walked to the front of the desk where Hessam was now standing. He slapped Hessam on the back and then announced, "I believe you've just solved the puzzle my friend."

Hessam looked at him with a look of astonishment. "Exactly what have I uncovered Erik?"

"Isn't it obvious that one, if not both of the guards must have known that the Red Diamond was not authentic? That would definitely explain why the two men are looking for it and why their lives would be in danger if the Shah ever found them."

"Although you may believe that the mystery has been solved, I don't have much hope that we'll ever know precisely what has transpired to lead to this predicament that I find myself in currently."

"Hessam, surely you realize that since I am in possession of the gem that it will be easier for us to coax that information from them. The only thing that bothers me is that the man I used to think of as ruthless and would sacrifice anything for his precious treasury hasn't made it public that his rare gem is missing. What he is hiding is the real mystery."

"Frankly, I'm not that interested in finding out Erik. I liked my life the way it was and even though I have enjoyed my time with you and your family, the time is fast approaching for Darius and me to get back to our lives."

"I would agree with you. That is why I'm devising a plan that will surely give you your life back."

At that time Amalie entered the room and announced that breakfast was ready and that Darius and Louisa were waiting patiently. Erik and Hessam cut their discussion short but promised to pick it up as soon as they could.

Disappearing Act

The next few months were full of family suppers with Chester, Meg, Isabel, Peter and their children. Erik relished in the time that he spent connecting with his father and Meg. It all seemed so surreal to him but so did every day after he had met Amalie. He and Chester had already become such great friends over the years that learning he was his father just solidified their friendship. It was hard to go from being friends to seeing him as a parental figure. Although in some ways Erik had always thought of him as a father, at their ages neither of them expected it to be a relationship like he had with his daughter Isabel or even Frederic for that matter. Their relationship was more of two men that were content to be in the company of one another; never having to express their thoughts about how they felt because they both already knew.

One afternoon Chester and Erik were sitting in front of the fireplace in the drawing room playing a game of chess and sipping their brandy when Hessam entered the room.

"Pardon the interruption gentlemen but Erik it is imperative that I speak to you."

"What about old friend?"

"I'd prefer that we speak in private," he insisted.

"Whatever you have to say Hessam can be spoken in front of Chester. You'll come to find that there are no secrets in this family. Secrets only tear down relationships and create distrust. You're among your friends and those that care about you. Speak freely. There will be no judgments made about you here."

"I assume then that he knows of my situation?"

"Yes he does and now would you please stop stalling. I'm in the process of deciding whether I should move my knight or my rook."

"I think that whatever your plans are for me that you should work quickly to put them into place. It is has been brought to my attention that the cellars have been drained of their water."

"Yes....I see....that does make the need for my plans to be expedited,"

~ 108 ~

he said as he rubbed his chin while he pushed his chair back and stood from his sitting position. "You'll have to excuse me Chester. It seems that I will need to ready myself for a trip to Paris."

"I'm going to go with you Erik," Chester boldly announced as he rose shakily from his seat. Erik put his hand on his father's shoulder and said, "Not this time. I need you to stay here and make sure that Meg, Amalie and Louisa are safe. Hessam and I will be able to handle this situation by ourselves. I don't want anyone to know that I have a family. It's better this way."

"But what if you need help son?"

"You're helping by staying here….that's all the help I'll need. Besides, Meg would never forgive me if I took you with me."

"And you think Amalie is going to be happy about this?"

"No, but she understands what it is that I have to do. That's why I love her so much."

"What you have to do is only necessary if……"

All of a sudden Amalie came running through the doors of the drawing room. She was hysterical and crying. "Erik, Erik, I'm so sorry… I took my eyes off of her for just a second and then….she was gone."

"What do you mean she was gone? Who was gone Amalie?"

"Louisa…..our precious Louisa is gone. She was playing in the stable…… while I was hanging the linens out to dry and then…….. I heard a scream and then silence. I ran to see what had happened and she was gone. I looked in the stalls and all around and then there it was, sitting there untouched, the comb… that was in her hair and this was with it." She handed Erik a piece of paper. He took it and read it quietly.

> *Hessam,*
>
> *If you are inclined to ever see the girl again I would impress upon you to follow my directions carefully. I have no plans to harm her unless you decide not to honor my wishes. You're a clever man Hessam and your staged drowning fooled me for quite some time however, it is best to never underestimate your adversaries especially when they know the same people as you.*
>
> *This is what I require of you. Meet me at the entrance to the cellars of the Paris Opera House on the Rue Scribe in three days before the sun sets. There you will take me into the cellar where Erik lived and grant me entrance into his home which I know that you have access to or you wouldn't still be alive. When I find what I am looking for the girl will be released to you, unharmed. However,*

*if I don't find what it is I'm searching for then it will be
your actions or lack thereof that will have sealed the girl's
fate. Bring no one with you and don't attempt to trick me
again.*
        Seeker of the Jewel

He gave it to Hessam and while he read it tears flowed from his
eyes. "I'm so sorry, Amalie......Erik. I should have never come here.
I should have never contacted my friends in Persia or Paris. I'm the
reason Louisa has been taken. I don't know how you'll ever forgive me
for this."

Erik held Amalie in his arms while she cried, barely able to breathe.
She knew she needed to calm down but she didn't think she would ever
be able to do so. Her daughter was in the hands of strangers; people
that were believed to be thieves and murderers. At this moment she
not only hated Hessam but Erik as well. She pulled herself away from
him and glared into his eyes. "This is your fault.....both of you. I may
never see my daughter again and it was all because of a worthless Red
Diamond and your pride. I hope you're both happy?" She stormed out
of the room and up the stairs.

Erik started to go after her but then decided that if he gave her
time to calm down he would likely be able to talk to her without an
argument ensuing. He looked at his friend who was beside himself with
guilt and grief. He put his hand on his shoulder as Hessam sat in the
chair with his head buried in his hands.

"Hessam, we've no time for regrets and pity. My daughter is out
there with two strange men and we must find her. Get Darius and your
things together. It seems that we will be going to Paris."

He wiped the tears from his eyes and stood up quickly. "You're
absolutely right Erik. We've no time to waste." He left the room and
walked up the stairs to the room where he and Darius had been staying.

"What can I do Erik?" asked Chester.

"You may ask Luc to get the horses hitched to the coach as quickly
as possible. Have Darius and Hessam on the coach to Paris as quickly
as you can. Luc is not to go with them. Have Darius steer the coach. I
need Luc to stay here with you, Amalie, Meg and Yvette. Get Amalie to
pack a bag of my things for me and have Hessam and Darius take them
to her uncle's flat. I'll meet them there as soon as I can. Tell them not to
leave the flat until I get there."

"Where are you going Erik?" Chester asked with concern in his voice.

"I'm going to find my daughter. Tell Amalie that I love her and I'll
see her soon." Erik walked out of the room and into the study to retrieve

his pistol. He then took his cloak and riding gloves from the closet and put them on.

"Erik you can't just go. You need to talk to Amalie," Chester pleaded.

"I've wasted valuable time already. They can't have gotten too far, especially if they are traveling by coach."

He ran out the front door and then down to the stable. He put Jasper's saddle on him and then climbed onto his back. As he turned to exit the stable doors Amalie stood in his path. Her eyes were red from crying and her face was pale.

"Erik, I'm sorry. I shouldn't have blamed you or Hessam."

"No Amalie, you're right. It's my fault and I owe it not just to Louisa but to you to make it right. I shouldn't have trusted that they wouldn't come here."

"You couldn't have known. Here......" she handed him two keys and then held his gloved hand against her face. "You'll need these when you reach Paris."

One key was to her uncle's flat and the other was to the bakery that was next to the opera house. He would need the one to the bakery to enter through the secret passage that they had used to exit the opera house all those years ago. He took them from her and kissed her hand.

"Thank you Amalie. I promise I'll bring her home to you or I won't come home. I love you."

"I love you too Erik. Go now before they get too far ahead of you. Please be careful."

He kicked Jasper in his flanks and he left through the stable doors like a bolt of lightning shoots from a cluster of clouds. It was obvious that the men were headed back to Paris so their trail should be easily picked up. He rode for an hour and began to wonder if he would ever see any signs of his daughter's captors. Although he saw no signs of a coach, there were several hoof prints that were freshly made that were headed toward a nearing village. Perhaps they were on horseback and hadn't planned far enough in advance to have secured a coach for their journey. He would need to keep a watchful eye out for any kind of travelers lest he miss his daughter.

He came to the village and dismounted his horse. He hoped that since it was nearing dusk that the men would stop for a meal and possibly try to find lodging that would provide them privacy so that no one would question why two men were traveling with a young girl. He walked through the town peering through café windows and asking the locals if they had seen two men of foreign decent. Being that his appearance was questionable too the willingness of the local people to help him dwindled quickly.

He continued to look around the village questioning the local villagers even though he knew it wouldn't produce any answers and then he came upon an old man who was begging for money. He had stopped a passerby to inquire if they had seen a young girl with two men and after the passerby left the beggar quietly said, "Why is this young girl so important to you?"

Erik spun around to find the old man pulling on his cloak while he tried to rise from his seated position. "She's my daughter, sir. Why do you ask? Have you seen her?"

"Son, I haven't seen anything since the day I was born but I have heard plenty. My ears don't fail me even when other parts of me do," he chuckled.

"Have you heard something about a young girl?"

"I haven't just heard about her, I know where she is."

"Tell me sir, please. Tell me."

"Why would you trust an old blind man?"

"Sir, if you could see me you would know why. Your blindness doesn't make you incapable of being trusted, it only makes you less likely to judge people by their appearance. You could almost argue that it makes you a more trustworthy person. Besides why would you lie to me about something so important?"

"Well, how do I know that you are truly her father and not someone who wants to take her from the people she's supposed to be with already?"

"You don't sir. You'll just have to take my word for it."

"And how much is your word worth? I've just met you and know nothing about your character."

"You're a wise man and I can see that getting you to trust that I am who I say I am will be a challenge that I don't have time for at the moment. However, if you can answer this one question for me it may answer your question about me."

"What is your question?"

"Was the girl talking when you crossed paths with her?"

"No, her words were muffled, like someone had their hands over her mouth."

"Does that answer your question about me?"

"Not exactly but it does make me believe that you aren't the one that is going to harm her."

"Then you'll tell me where she is?"

"No......I'll show you." The old man grabbed Erik's arm with his left hand and took his stick in the other waving it as he walked by objects so that he wouldn't hit them as he walked. He took Erik down the main street and then turned right, leading him onto a path that led to the blacksmith's workshop. He stopped suddenly, listening. He then pointed his stick in the direction of a small cottage that was across the street from the blacksmith's workshop.

"That is where your daughter is. The blacksmith takes money from travelers and allows them to stay in his home while he stays in his workshop."

"Thank you. I owe you my daughter's life." Erik took out his money clip, pulled several francs from its clasp and put them into the man's hand. "I will come see you again in a few weeks and make sure that you are properly cared for but for now please take this as a token of my thanks. God bless you sir."

"I didn't help you for a reward young man. I did it because it was the right thing to do. I can't accept your gift." He handed it back to Erik.

"But this will buy you food, clothes and some shelter from the cold winter days and nights. Please sir, take it." He put it back into the man's hand.

"God has always provided for me young man," the old man said as he tried to give Erik back the money.

"Yes, I'm sure He has and today He has provided you with me. Are you going to tell God that you don't like how He is providing for you today?"

The old man was taken aback by Erik's bold but wise words. He took the money and placed it in his tattered coat pocket and said, "No, I suppose I shouldn't question His methods or means of providing for me. It's been years since He has sent me anyone that knew Him as well as I do."

"Then I would say that we have both been blessed this evening. Take care of yourself sir and again, thank you." Erik shook the man's hand and then politely excused himself from their conversation. The old man turned and went back to the street where he had been sitting.

Erik was glad that the cover of darkness was soon upon them and it would create the best circumstances to descend upon the small cottage where he believed his daughter was being held against her will. He went back to where he had left Jasper and took him to the blacksmith's shop. He knocked on the door of the workshop and a tall muscular man opened the door.

"We're closed sir."

"I'm not looking to have the horse shoed. I was told that you rent rooms to travelers. Would you happen to have a room available this evening?" Erik asked as he pulled the collar of his cloak up to shield his mask from the view of the blacksmith.

"No sir, I've just rented my small cottage to two men and their cousin's daughter. If you ask me, I don't think she's a relative at all but I've learned not to ask too many questions."

"I see. Would you mind if I stayed in your workshop?"

"My workshop isn't for rent but I have a stall in the stable you are welcome to sleep in, if you don't mind sleeping with the horses."

"That will be fine. I'll only need to rest for a couple of hours and then I'll be on my way. Would it be too much to ask if I can feed and water my horse too? I'll pay of course."

"Certainly, I'll take the money now and then you're free to do as you wish."

Erik handed him several francs and the man handed him a lantern that was lit so that he could see his way. He led Jasper to the stable and unsaddled him. He was pleased that the man was so agreeable. This was the perfect place to keep a watchful eye on the men who had taken Louisa.

Inside the cottage the men were smoking their cigars while Louisa sat in the corner of the room crying, scared, bound and gagged. Her head was buried in her knees and she sat silently praying for her mother and father to find her. She didn't want to be scared but she was. However, she knew that being scared wouldn't help her out of her current situation. She continued to pray for God to give her strength and to help her not be scared. The more she prayed the more she felt at peace. Her mother had always told her when she was scared that God was always there to help. All she would need to do was call upon Him. While she prayed silently her stomach began to rumble. She was hungry and desperately wanted to go home. The door opened and the blacksmith came through the door with food for the three of them. He never noticed that Louisa was bound or gagged since they had ordered her to keep her head down and in her hood and her arms under her cloak whenever anyone else was around. When the blacksmith left, Danush walked over to Louisa and pulled her to her feet.

"You need to eat girl." He drug her to a chair at the table and pushed her into it. He then took her gag from her mouth. She looked at her hands and then at her fork and spoon.

"I need to have my hands untied if I'm going to eat."

"Did you say something?" Danush asked angrily.

Louisa didn't know why she said it but she repeated her words again but this time with more force and purpose. "You'll need to untie my hands if you expect me to eat. I'm not going to eat like an animal."

He grabbed her hands, jerking her toward him and she stared him in the eyes with no fear. "Is that so?" Danush said to her.

"Yes, it is," she replied back to him.

He took out his knife and put it between her wrists and cut the rope off of her hands. "You've got a lot of fight in you. I would keep my mouth shut if you want to keep it all in one piece girl."

She gave him an angry stare and then began eating. The men took their plates and sat in front of the small fireplace eating their meals ignoring her. Louisa took this opportunity to scan the room for any possible way of escape. She noticed that the door only had one latch and one lock. The latch was low and easily handled and the lock had not been pulled down yet. Her father had taught her a thing or two about not being the victim of anyone else's plans. She knew she was only six years old but she also knew that no matter her age she could still find a way to get out. Her father had always told her that knowledge and persistence were the best weapons against anyone. If you had all of the weapons in the world but didn't know how to use them, they would be useless. That is why he encouraged her to learn something new every day. It wasn't the size of the person that mattered it was using what God had given you and trusting that God would use it to help you. He would then remind her of David and Goliath and at that moment she was definitely identifying with David. The two men were discussing who would take watch first to make sure she didn't escape and she was hoping that it would be Fardin. He didn't seem to be as wicked or cross with her. She overheard them saying that she was a child and once she fell asleep she wouldn't wake until they woke her. She had decided that it wouldn't get to that point.

After she cleaned her plate of any food that had once been on it, she put her hands in her cloak pockets and pulled out the flint and two bags of the magic powder. The two men were so involved in their planning that they didn't notice her working feverishly to get the flint to ignite the fuses of the two bags. She had moved her chair slowly away from the table and positioned herself where her back was facing the men. Before they knew what had happened a bright flash of red and orange light lit up the small room. She managed to get to the door and unlatch it as the cloud of smoke filled the air and kept the men from seeing her leave. After she exited she ran toward the stable where she believed she could hide until she could figure out a way to get back to her home in Trie-Chateau.

Erik had been watching the cottage and when he saw the flash of light and saw the smoke billowing out the front door, he knew that Louisa had conjured the best magic trick that she knew how in order to escape. He opened the stable door and began immediately putting Jasper's saddle on him. He spotted Louisa running toward the stable as the moon lit up the night sky briefly until another cloud covered its illumination. Erik could hear the two men choking and coughing as they exited the house. He waited inside the stable until she was safely inside. He put his right arm around her waist, pulling her to him and covered her mouth with his other hand so that she wouldn't scream; alerting the men to her whereabouts.

"Louisa, you're safe," he whispered. It's your father."

She threw her arms around him and began to cry. "I was so scared Father."

"But you were so brave too Louisa." He kissed her on her forehead and hugged her tightly. "I'm so glad you're all right. Now, I have one more thing I need you to do Louisa. Can you be brave for me one more time?"

"I think so Father."

"I need you to throw your voice toward the blacksmith's shop. Can you do that for me?"

"What do you want me to say?"

"Scream for help, Louisa. Just make them believe you are near the blacksmith's shop."

He picked up Louisa and sat her on top of Jasper and then climbed up and sat behind her on the saddle. Jasper walked to the edge of the stable doors where they could both see the two men looking in the darkness to see where she had gone.

"Now, Louisa. Do your best."

She threw her voice toward the workshop and it echoed through the valley. The men changed their direction and headed toward the voice. Erik slowly rode Jasper out the back of the stable and into the field that paralleled the cottage. He then found a path that led into the streets of the small village and then onto the main thoroughfare. From that point on, they rode quickly into the darkness toward their home.

They rode blindly into the night with the glow of the moon's light only showing their path periodically. As the time neared midnight they reached the chateau. Louisa had fallen asleep, nestled in her father's chest.

"Louisa, we're home," he whispered in his daughter's ear trying to awaken her.

Amalie, who had been unable to sleep, was in the kitchen watching Sampson lap up a bowl of milk. She had begun making dough when she heard the front door open and close. She ran to the foyer and there she found Erik holding a sleeping Louisa in his arms. She ran to them and kissed them both.

"You're all right! You're both all right!" she said as tears of joy streamed down her cheeks. "Come; let's get you both by the fire to warm you up. I'll bring her bed clothes and change her down here while you go up and change for bed."

Amalie went up the stairs and returned with Louisa's bed clothes and Erik instead of going up to change went into the kitchen, the study, and then into the drawing room. Amalie finished dressing Louisa and left her sleeping on the sofa with several blankets draped over her. She wouldn't sleep in her room tonight and neither would Amalie. She planned on staying next to her daughter so that when she woke she would be there for her.

Erik walked out of the drawing room with a disappointed and puzzled look on his face.

"Amalie, where's Chester? I instructed him to stay here with you and make sure you were safe."

Amalie went over to him and entwined her arm with his walking him to the bottom of the staircase. "I'm afraid that you're not going to like what I'm about to tell you. You're father left with Hessam and Darius. I tried to make him stay but he insisted that you would need him."

"That's perfect Amalie. Now I not only have Hessam to worry about but I have to worry about Chester too."

"I never hear you say that you're concerned about Darius. Why is that?"

"Because Darius does as he is told, always has. I wish my father was more like him."

"Unfortunately my love, I think it is you who are like your father. I've never known you to do what you were told either. The similarities between the two of you aren't just in the way you look."

"So it would seem. However, it doesn't help my situation. What did Meg say when he left with them?"

"She was as I always am, understanding but concerned. She couldn't deny him his wish to help his son. Not after all the years he wasn't able to help you."

Erik dropped his head and sighed deeply. "As a father I can understand his motives and the emotions that led him to his decision and I would have done the same. Nevertheless, his actions have left me with no one to look after you, Meg and the others."

"Do you think that they'll come back to the house to get Louisa?"

"It's not likely since they have instructed Hessam to meet them in three days and the trip to and from Paris takes a full day if not more. They probably won't waste their time coming back here but I'd rather make sure you were protected than to depend on my own assumptions. After all the men we are dealing with are desperate."

"I think we'll be all right if we stay here but if it will make you feel better we'll go to Isabel's first thing in the morning. I'll make sure that we all stay together until you return," Amalie assured him.

"I knew you would understand. Now I'm going to get some rest so that I can get an early start on my trip to Paris tomorrow. You sent my things with the others I trust?"

"Yes and I also took the liberty of packing my father's sgian-dhu in your bag as well. It will be easily concealed inside your boot."

He kissed her on the lips and then embraced her. "I can always count on you to anticipate anything I need. Thank you."

"You're welcome. Now get some rest. I'm going to stay with Louisa."

He stepped lively up the stairs and out of sight as Amalie returned to her daughter's side. She sat on the floor next to her stroking her hair as she slept. She laid her head on the edge of the sofa and said a prayer, thanking God for the safe return of her child and husband. She knew that Erik and the others would also need his protection in the days to come and prayed for His watchful and merciful hand to be upon them. Her eyes became heavy and then her head slowly tilted and met the blankets that covered Louisa. She could no longer fight the slumber that awaited her. Her eyes closed as she gave her daughter's hand one more kiss and her head rested gently on the edge of the sofa where she finally found peaceful sleep.

She's Gone

Fardin and Danush spent the majority of the evening looking for Louisa. They prowled through the village asking anyone they came upon if they had seen a young girl traveling alone. No one could recall seeing anyone that matched her description nor did they seem to care if they found her. There was no offer from anyone to help find her and the only person that could have answered their questions was ignored. After all how could a blind man help them?

They returned to the cottage after the smoke cleared and the blacksmith was standing inside waiting for them. The small explosion had left a charred mark on the wood floor the size of a plate and the smoke left a scent that was displeasing to the senses.

"What happened here?" the blacksmith demanded.

Fardin stumbled over his words and cowered behind Danush as he spoke. "We had a slight accident. I was smoking my cigar and carelessly set it down on a dish towel which ignited it. I threw it on the floor and tried stomping it out but it didn't work. Eventually it burned out, leaving the mark on the floor."

The blacksmith looked at the men and then the floor. He could tell they were lying but honestly didn't want to know any more than what he already knew. "Where is the girl?"

The men exchanged glances and then Danush answered, "We took her into the village and paid a barmaid to look after her until the smoke cleared. We were coming back to see if it was safe for us to return so that we may all get some sleep."

"Sir, there are no establishments open at this hour and I demand to know why you feel that you must lie to me?"

"It's quite embarrassing sir and I'm ashamed to admit it but the girl has run away......are you happy now? She obviously wanted to go back to my cousin's house. We searched everywhere for her and she is nowhere to be found. It's like she disappeared into thin air."

"Did you search the stable?"

"Yes."

"Did you speak to the gentleman that was sleeping there?"

"There wasn't anyone there when we searched the stable. What did this man look like?" Danush asked the blacksmith.

"He was tall, had a rather low voice and I couldn't tell you much more than that since I didn't see his face. He kept his cloak collar pulled up high where I couldn't see him. The wind was blowing rather wildly so I figured he was just trying to keep warm."

"Did he say who he was or where he was going?"

"No, just that he needed to rest for a few hours and to feed and water his horse," the blacksmith said with a matter of fact tone.

Danush thought that it was strange that a man would stay for such a brief period of time but didn't believe that he had anything to do with the disappearance of the girl. Fardin had only reported to Danush that Hessam and Darius were staying with some friends in Trie-Chateau. He didn't know anything about the family friends just that they had a daughter and that Hessam was rather fond of her. No, Hessam wouldn't risk the girl's life by following them and trying to bring her back before their planned meeting. That would be out of character for him. This was purely a coincidence.

"I doubt he has anything to do with it. I'm almost certain that the girl is hiding in a barn or cellar in the village somewhere. It makes no difference to me. She'll have to come out and show herself eventually. We'll find her." Danush said as he rubbed the scar underneath his eye.

"I hope she does for your sakes but my only concern now is collecting payment for the damage you have done to my cottage."

Danush put his hand into his pocket and pulled out several francs and handed it to the blacksmith. "Will this be enough?"

He looked at what had been handed to him and answered, "Consider your debt paid. Good night gentlemen. I do hope you find the little girl. If I see her I'll send her to you."

"Thank you that would be most helpful."

Fardin shut the door and then took a deep breath. He looked at Danush with a concerned look on his face and asked, "What if we don't find the girl? What will we do then?"

"We'll carry out our plans; that's what we'll do. Hessam doesn't know that we don't have the girl so he will meet us like we have instructed him to do. Just his believing that we have the girl will give us the upper hand."

Fardin smiled and then took a seat, propping his feet upon the table. "Then I guess we'll have our Red Diamond and he'll have nothing."

"Precisely!" he said as he opened the door to the back room of the cottage. "I'm going to get some sleep now. Lock the door and make sure you put another log on the fire."

Fardin nodded, acknowledging his colleague's request. He then added another piece of wood to the fire, locked the door, threw his bedding on the floor and stretched out on top of it. He stared at the ceiling for a while and then closed his eyes and quickly fell asleep.

One More Finale

*E*rik reached Paris with only a day left from the deadline. Although he was tired from his journey he didn't make his way to the flat where his friends awaited him. Instead he boarded Jasper at the livery stables and made his way to the alley behind the bakery. He waited until the owner locked up for the night and left to go home before he entered using the key that Amalie had given to him. It amazed him that the key still worked after all this time. He said a quick prayer and then ventured into the storage cellar where the secret door to his lake house was hidden. He searched for the lantern that had hung nearby and found that it was in its place. He lit it and then found the mechanism that allowed him entrance. He brushed the cobwebs away from his face as he made his way down the steps that led to the retractable drainage grate. He could feel the frigid water through his boots as he stepped on the sunken stone that led him into the main tunnel. When he reached the secret door that separated him from his lake house and the tunnel, he took a deep breath and pushed the small stone that shifted the lever that released the door. It slowly opened and he quickly made his way into the place he used to call home.

He walked down into the main room and saw that all was as he had left it except for a chair that had been moved by Hessam months before when he had entered. He set the lantern down and began lighting candles and other lanterns so that he could see to begin his work. When he came to the room where his organ still sat, he noticed his sword sitting beside it. He picked it up and examined it, then put the leather strap that would hold it in place around his waist. It was possible that he may have a need for such a weapon. He had less than twenty-two hours left to prepare for his visitors. He knew exactly what needed to be done and hoped that it would be enough to keep these two men from ever trying to hurt his family again.

It was close to nine o'clock in the evening and Hessam was growing impatient. Where was Erik and why hadn't he arrived yet? Then he heard a key turning in the door. He grabbed his pistol and readied himself to fire. The door opened slowly and Erik walked into the room to find Hessam pointing his pistol at him.

"Good heavens man, put that away. You mustn't point your pistol at people if you don't intend to fire it."

"Oh, I had every intention of firing it if it wasn't you. Where have you been? We've been waiting for a day and a half for you to arrive."

"I've been busy returning my daughter to her mother," he answered with a smile.

"She's safe?" Hessam inquired.

"Yes. No thanks to me. She's quite clever and managed to free herself. I was just glad that I was there to pick her up and take her home."

"Well that doesn't surprise me at all. Her mother is a bit of an adventurer as well as her father," Hessam laughed as he slapped him on the back.

"She comes by it naturally I suppose. Speaking of which, where is my father?"

"He's resting in the bedroom. The trip nearly broke him Erik. We tried to convince him to stay home but he insisted on driving the coach and coming along to help you. Now I know why you are so stubborn."

"I don't think it is passed on from generation to generation, I think it is who he is and who am I to question that? He'll be all right as long as he stays here at the flat." He turned to Darius and spoke. "I want you to make sure he stays here with you. You both need to stay out of sight until three hours after the time that we are to meet with the two men. Then I would like you to bring my horse, a wagon and the coach to the Rue Scribe and wait for us. Do you understand?"

Darius nodded in his direction acknowledging that he understood what he and Chester were to do. Then Erik instructed Hessam on what it was he was to do once he met with the two men. He had just begun informing them that he wouldn't be staying with them at the flat for the evening when Chester entered the room.

"Erik, did you find Louisa? Is she safe?" Chester asked.

"Yes, Chester and she is at home with her mother which is where I specifically requested you to stay."

"I couldn't let you come here to face these evil men alone. You're my son and I want to help you."

"Your enthusiasm and willingness to help is duly noted but Chester.....Father, pardon my directness, your age has rendered you feeble and your reactions aren't as quick or sharp as they once were. I don't want anything to happen to you."

"I understand son but you must let me help you. I owe it to you."

"You owe me nothing Father. You never had a debt to me that needed to be paid. God has seen fit to give us time together. Let's not trifle over things that don't matter." Erik put his arm around his shoulder and walked him to the small sofa in the sitting room.

"I have given you and Darius an important task and you must promise me that you won't stray from my instructions. Do you understand me?"

Chester sat quietly not saying anything and then answered with a disagreeable tone in his voice, "Yes, Erik…..I understand."

"If it all works out the way I have planned there won't ever be a need to speak of the Red Diamond of Nadirijna again."

Erik made each of them recite back to him what it was they were to do so that everything would go as he had planned. He then went to the room where his things were and gathered up all that he would need along with his sgian-dhu and placed it inside his boot. He was just about to exit the flat when the door knob rattled. Someone was trying to gain entry. Hessam pulled his pistol as the others scattered to the outskirts of the room out of the line of sight from anyone coming through the door. Erik approached the door with his pistol drawn and then slowly turned the knob and flung open the door with his pistol pointed directly at the face of the man that stood waiting outside.

"Peter?" he exclaimed. "What in heaven's name are you doing here?"

"Are you going to shoot me or invite me in out of this drafty corridor?"

"Come in, come in," Erik said as he holstered his pistol and shut the door behind him.

"I was relying on you to take care of my wife as well as yours and the children."

"Yes, I'm sure you were. However your wife and sister insisted on me coming to help you. Besides you forgot something that was very important and Amalie insisted that I bring it to you."

"And what might that be?"

Peter reached into his pocket and pulled out a small black pouch and a skeleton key. He handed them to Erik as the others watched.

"She said to tell you that she was sorry but she forgot to give it to Hessam to give to you. She also said that the Red Diamond of Nadirijna needed to return home and that this time your pride shouldn't get in the way of it returning."

That sounds exactly like something my adoring wife would say. Unfortunately, I don't think the Shah wants it back."

"What do you mean Erik?"

"The two men, Danush, who has the scar and Fardin aren't worried about returning the diamond to the Shah; they are interested in keeping it for themselves."

"How do you know this?" Hessam asked inquisitively. "And how do you know their names?"

"Did you forget that Louisa was with them for several hours? She is a typical six year old who likes to listen to conversations she isn't supposed to hear. She provided me with some very useful information."

Peter sat on the sofa next to Hessam and Chester after he greeted them.

"Well, are you planning on keeping this information to yourself or are you going to share it with us?" Peter said with a sarcastic tone in his voice.

"Not all of it was understandable. Louisa tends to add to the stories she overhears. It does seem however, that this time she has probably not embellished it at all." He paced around the room flipping the skeleton key between his fingers. They all waited anxiously for him to spill the contents from the jar of mystery so that they could see what lie at the bottom of it.

"Louisa overheard them planning to take the Red Diamond to a black market merchant and then use the money to go to America. It seems that the Shah had employed Danush to steal it by giving him access to it by way of the secret tunnel that led into the treasury room. He was then supposed to replace it with a jewel that was to look like the Red Diamond so that the Shah could wear it without being a victim of the curse. Of course, Louisa didn't tell me this in these exact words but from the bits and pieces she told me I was able to figure it out.

Once Danush had taken it far away, he was to bring it back to the palace and affix it to the ornate throne that was adorned with so many jewels it would never be noticed but its value would still be a part of the treasures of Persia. Danush and Fardin stopped speaking once they realized that she was listening to them but this is what I believe to have happened next." Erik continued to pace around the room, checked the time on his pocket watch and then went to the foyer closet and retrieved his cloak. He pulled on his cloak and gloves as he continued.

"I believe that Danush became greedy and decided to run away with the jewel. When the Shah realized that he wasn't going to return, he involved yet another guard. He sent him to retrieve Danush but didn't tell him about the jewel. When the two men met and Danush's life was about to be snuffed out I believe he made a deal with his assassin to give him part of the proceeds after they sold the gem; an offer that Fardin couldn't refuse. However, upon selling the gem they found that it wasn't a Red Diamond but a well-disguised ruby in which they now possessed. When the second guardsman didn't return, the Shah couldn't tell anyone else and therefore to protect himself from ever being found out, he locked up the room to keep them out if they decided to return. The Shah wasn't that interested in the Red Diamond, he was only interested in what the two men knew. The Red Diamond is of no consequence to him. The gem that he wears now will not be discovered to be anything less than what he claims it to be until he is dead."

Peter rubbed his chin and then stood from where he was sitting and walked over to Erik. "How does any of this help our situation?" Peter asked putting his hands on Erik's shoulders.

"It provides us with the motives of these two men and it reveals not just what they are afraid of but whom. Exploiting a man's weakness is always easier when you know what it is Peter," he smiled as he put his hat on his head.

"Where are you going Erik?"

"I've got things to do and I must make certain that the lake house is suitable for my visitors tomorrow. Besides, I must enter through the bakery before the bakers arrive."

"I'm going with you. It's not safe for you to go alone at this time of night." Peter collected his hat, gloves and overcoat.

"If I thought it would do any good I would insist that you stay put but I haven't the energy or the time to argue with you. Do as I tell you, when I tell you and you'll make it home to your wife and children."

Peter chuckled at his words and slapped him on the back as they exited through the door. "Your deep concern for me is why I cherish our friendship so much. There's no need to be so dramatic."

Erik spun around on his heels as they walked to the entrance of the building and looked into Peter's eyes with a seriousness he had not seen in a long time. "This is no game Peter. These men are trained royal guards and they are dangerous. I don't take anything lightly so if I'm dramatic it's only because I value your life and those that we have left at home. If we don't put an end to this here and now they won't stop until they get what they want. I, for one, would like to spend my old age sitting in that office of ours drafting grand chateaus for wealthy men who don't know how else to spend their money. I've had to look over my shoulder most of my life and I'm done with it. I don't want my family or yours for that matter, to ever have a need to live like that."

Peter was surprised by the passion of Erik's words. He could tell that coming to Paris had brought back many memories and feelings; none in which he could find solace or joy.

"You're right and I'm sorry. I understand the seriousness of what is about to transpire."

"It's all right Peter. I know that you deflect your fear by making light of dangerous situations. I know that if you had a choice you would rather be at home."

"And you would rather be there too," Peter said as he checked his pistol to make sure it was secure in its holster.

"Yes, but then who would help Hessam? I'm actually looking forward to one more finale at the opera house. It's been a long time since the Opera Ghost has haunted the cellars."

They made their way onto the streets of Paris and began walking toward the part of the city where the opera house was located.

"Are you telling me that he is about to be resurrected?" Peter asked while he pulled his overcoat tightly over his chest to prevent the cold air from slicing him like a knife.

"He'll only be alive for a couple of hours and only for a special audience. I have no intentions of making our presence known there. That's why we are entering through the bakery tonight."

"Tell me, what does the skeleton key unlock?" Peter curiously asked.

"It's not what it unlocks it's what it locks up that will be useful to us."

"And what exactly is that?"

"It is best that you're unaware of such a thing Peter until it is time for it to be known."

They walked until they reached the bakery and then Erik led Peter down into the belly of the opera house. Erik walked him up a very long flight of stairs and instructed him not to move forward only backward if he needed to move at all. Peter couldn't see but an arm's length in front of him since Erik had taken the lantern. Then after a few minutes of waiting Erik joined him at the top of the ledge with a lantern which provided him enough light to see the edge of the lake from the vantage point he was provided. He was glad Erik had instructed him not to move forward because had he stepped one foot further he would have fallen from the top of the bulkhead walls and plunged directly into the landing below. Peter scanned the vast area and as he looked down he could see the winding staircase that came halfway up the bulkhead wall and ended abruptly; leading nowhere. At least that is how it looked.

"What do you think of my former residence?" Erik inquired.

"It's dark, damp and unbelievably cold but other than that I think you should take holiday here at least twice a year," Peter sarcastically commented. "How did you ever manage to stay sane living down here?" Erik looked at him with disapproval in his eyes and then Peter recanted, "Never mind, you don't have to answer that. I'm surprised that no one ever found their way in here."

"Oh they found their way to the lake but never into my home. I made sure that it was sealed as tight as a drum before I left. In fact the ledge you're standing on is only visible from this vantage point. If you were standing on the edge of the lake, the wall above you would appear to be connected to the wall you are standing upon now. Illusions were something I took great time in creating and I would say that they worked well."

"Weren't you afraid that the water would ever flow over your wall when the water table rose?"

"You underestimate my engineering Peter. I'm hurt," he laughed. "The wall is approximately fifteen meters from the shore of the lake to where you are standing. The water would never rise more than nine meters even after a thunderous rain storm. Besides I designed the ledge to be a trough that would collect the water and then spill into the stairs that is also a trough. At the bottom of the staircase there is a grate that allows the water to flow into a drainage canal that runs underneath the opera house and empties out into the street drains."

"It appears that you thought of everything."

"Not everything just the things I needed to survive."

Peter continued to look around noticing that Erik's former lair was full of many things that would need explanation.

"Where does that staircase lead?" Peter pointed to the winding stairs that wound against the outside bulkhead wall.

"It doesn't lead anywhere. I constructed it to be a decoy to deter anyone from finding where the real doors are located."

"And where would that be Erik?"

"There's one in the second landing of the staircase and one underneath the staircase."

Peter looked at him not understanding what he had just been told.

"I would use the one under the staircase to exit when I wanted to go for walks on the Rue Scribe and to run errands in the city. The one on the landing is a trap door; put there for protection as well as quick entry. Otherwise I would enter through the stables and then make my way to the secret door on the third floor. From there I could go anywhere I wanted to go inside the opera house."

"Weren't you afraid that they would see you?"

"They saw me many times but since this is a place where most of the people are in costume, they didn't notice me. When I wanted them to see me they would see me. That is why my living here was so ideal."

"If I didn't know better I would say that you enjoyed deceiving those around you."

"Yes, I suppose I did. It was my choice of entertainment. I never wished to harm anyone. I only wished to be left alone with my music." Erik closed his eyes and could almost hear the music from the opera house resonating in his ear. Then he felt Peter's hand on his shoulder and it brought him back to the present.

"Do you miss the life you had here?"

"Never! This was a prison not a home. I only miss the music and even that is easily dismissed since the music that soothed me in the dark was a reflection of my empty soul and it is no longer what I seek to comfort me." He led Peter down the stairs that had led him to the ledge of the bulkhead wall. He continued to show Peter all of the rooms in the lake house except for one. Peter marveled at the level of intricate detail that Erik had put into the place he had once lived.

"This place is every bit as captivating as you described it. Your talents were definitely not wasted."

"Thank you. That means a lot coming from you."

Peter walked over to the door that separated him from the room Erik had not shown him.

"What secrets do you keep behind this door?" he said as he turned the knob hoping it would open.

Erik peered at him across the room as he fumbled with some wire and a small box.

"Not anything in which you need to concern yourself, Peter. Sometimes it is best not to look behind locked doors because what you may find may not be what you hoped would be there."

"Always the riddles come from your mouth when it is something that you don't wish me to know about you or your former life. Why is that Erik?"

"I don't know what you mean. I'm not hiding anything."

"Then let me look behind your locked door."

He threw the skeleton key to Peter from where he was sitting and said in a very calm voice, "Be my guest but don't say that I didn't warn you."

Peter took the key, put it in the lock and turned it. He slowly pushed the door open and walked into the room. As he entered he could feel the temperature in the room rise, the mirrors that surrounded him projected his likeness as well as the reflection of the iron tree that was in the room. He looked up to see the source of the heat which was three very large lights pointed directly into the room. As his eyes continued upward he saw a black hole with a lip that jutted slightly over the wall of the room. He couldn't imagine what its use was and then he saw the most horrific of sights that troubled him greatly. He saw not one but two Punjab lassos hanging from the iron tree. It startled him and he fell backward into one of the mirrored walls. The heat that radiated off the surface burned him and he quickly jumped away from it. He exited the room abruptly because of the sweltering heat that was overcoming him. He shut the door and turned the key locking the door behind him. Then he joined Erik in the main room where he was seated on a beautifully upholstered sofa. The fabric was a shade of green that was as brilliant as an emerald and the covered buttons that were fastened to it were the color of gold. Erik continued to work; never looking up once to see the expression on Peter's face.

Handing Erik the key he said, "I should have taken your advice and not looked into that room. I'm not sure as to what purpose that room serves but then again I'm also not certain that I truly want to know."

Erik continued to work not saying a word. His silence was curious but Peter knew that when he was ready he would either explain or dismiss its existence completely. Minutes passed and Peter examined all of the interesting figurines, tapestries and other pieces of furniture that aligned the walls and floors. Erik still continued to work without making a sound.

"Why would Amalie think you would need the skeleton key? Does she have any idea what it unlocks?" Peter asked trying to get Erik to speak.

Erik continued to sit in silence; not acknowledging a word that Peter uttered.

"Good heavens Erik are you going to torture me with your silence the rest of the night?"

Erik picked his head up and fixed his eyes on Peter.

"Torturing you was not my intention but since we are on the subject that is what the room is made to do," Erik said with no hint of emotion detected in his voice.

"And Amalie knew that the key opened that door?" Peter asked again.

"Yes, she did. She also knows that it not only opens the door to the torture chamber but it also opens all of the doors in the opera house." Erik took what he had been working on and placed it on the table that was next to the sofa. Then he pulled a chair up and sat directly in front of Peter. His eyes were tired and Peter could tell that there was something that he needed to tell him.

"Peter, we've been friends for a while now and you're aware of the man that I used to be. I have prayed that I would never have a need to return to the ways of my former self but it seems that our current situation presents a dilemma. Although I am obligated to protect my family, I don't wish to take anyone's life in order to do so, but it may come to that. As you know, my list of indiscretions is long and I'll never be able to erase what has already happened. Knowing how that has impacted my life I cannot in my good conscience ask you to participate in the plans that I have made for the two men that will enter this glorified mausoleum." Erik stared into Peter's eyes waiting for a response.

"Erik, I have no problem with shedding blood as long as it isn't mine," he said as he smiled at his very somber colleague.

"That's just it Peter, I can't guarantee that your blood won't be shed or worse. You asked me what the use of the room was and I feel that I must tell you that what happens in that room won't be pleasant for its inhabitants. It's not a room that any man will ever walk out of unless I grant them the permission to do so. It's designed to cause a man to lose his faculties and in his quest for relief from the heat and delusions he will eventually kill himself by using the Punjab lasso that has been provided for him or even worse he will die of thirst."

"I know that you're concerned for my wellbeing but I wouldn't have come had I not considered the danger involved. I'm quite capable of handling a pistol and a sword if you must know. Who do you think has been instructing Isabel to fire her pistol?"

"I see. You've been holding out on me."

"No, just waiting for the right time to tell you. I wouldn't want you to exploit my talents," Peter said while he tried to contain his laughter at his own words. "If your plan is to get these two men into the chamber then how is it that you believe that there may not be any blood shed or life extinguished?"

"I had hoped that maybe you would be able to help me with that."

"Why can't you just give them what they want Erik? Give them the Red Diamond and then let them go on their way. They'll never have to know that you're still alive."

"I thought about that, believe me....many times. It sounds like a good plan but then what is to stop these two men from killing Hessam and then telling everyone how to get into the lake house."

"The lake house is of no consequence but as far as Hessam is concerned, I see what you mean. They're likely to kill him once they get what they have come to take." Peter rose from his seat and began pacing. "I thought you told Amalie you were going to get rid of the gem?"

"I said that I would do my best to rid us of this cursed jewel. I never said I was going to give it to the two men that threatened Hessam and kidnapped my child. I still intend on sending it far away."

"Then where do you plan on sending it?"

"That is a question that only the two men that seek it will be able to answer."

"Erik I would truly like to sit here and listen to your riddles but I'm afraid that sleep is what my body requires at this time. If it is all right with you I'll take the bed in the small room."

"Help yourself. I'll sleep on the sofa," Erik said as he fluffed the small pillow that leaned against the arm.

Erik settled onto the sofa and Peter made his way into the small room that had a beautiful bed with white linens draped on them except the dust had settled on the top turning them yellow. Peter shook the dust from the blanket and then returned it to the bed. He sat on the edge of the bed, removed his boots and as he rose from placing them on the floor he saw something tucked under a doily on the nightstand. He picked up the edge of the fragile paper and pulled it out to have a look at it. It was a small picture of a young girl with her mother and father. He didn't recognize any of the people in the picture and wondered who they could be. It was so strange to see it sitting there but he didn't dare bring attention to it. He would save his questions as to why it was there for another day. He tucked it back under the doily and climbed into the bed.

Heart's Desire

The morning came but Erik and Peter were unaware of it. The soli-
tude of the cellar kept any daylight from finding its way into the
inner realm where they were sleeping comfortably. It was almost noon
before Erik woke. Erik began his day by checking to make sure that all
of the trap doors were working properly and that the wiring that connected to the lights above the chamber was in working order as well.
He didn't want anything to go wrong.

Peter woke and found Erik sitting beside his bed staring at him.
When he saw that Peter was awake he looked at his pocket watch, not-
ing that the hour was now twenty-one minutes past three. Sunset would
be in approximately two hours or less.

"I was wondering when you might decide to join me." Erik said as
he put his watch back into his vest pocket.

"Had you not kept me up so late with your riddles I wouldn't have
needed so much sleep. What time is it, anyway?"

"Sunset will be here in less than three hours. We have only a short
time to prepare ourselves for our guests." Erik said as he rose from his
chair, pushing it back under the dressing table.

"Is there anything to eat? I'm famished." Peter asked as he pulled his
boots onto his feet.

"There are some pastries on the table in the main room. I helped
myself to the ones that the baker saw fit to toss out; apparently if it is a
day old it not suitable for the patrons."

"Did you remove them from the garbage?"

"No, I removed them from his storage room. He always keeps what
is left and gives it to the needy. I would say that we fit that description
today."

"You're quite resourceful."

"Yes and it seems that I have also developed a conscience."

"How do you mean?"

"I put a few coins in the baker's till for our daily bread. I couldn't
take it without knowing that I had paid for it. It's strange that only seven

years ago I would have taken it with very little consideration for who it may affect. And now today I am still struggling with what it is I'm about to do."

"Remember my friend it wasn't you who began this test of wills."

"Wasn't it though? I'm the one who took something that didn't belong to me in the first place which has now caused an unbelievable series of events that may lead to loss of life. Amalie was right when she said that it was my pride that had caused all of this."

"Perhaps but you can't undo what is already done. You can only try to make it right Erik." Peter put his hand on Erik's shoulder as they walked into the main room. "I don't know many men that would come to the aid of a friend whose life was in danger. Whether you can keep from spilling blood today will matter not on what you do but on how the other two men react to a dead man's proposition."

Erik smiled at Peter and took a seat on the sofa. He picked up the plate of pastries and offered it to his friend. Peter took a few pastries and began eating them slowly. A pot of warm water was sitting on the table as well. The two men made their tea and drank it as if there was nothing out of the ordinary looming in the hours to come. They spent the rest of their time talking and even praying together. They knew they would need more than their own strength and cunning to make it safely to the next daybreak.

The hour came when Hessam was to meet the two men on the Rue Scribe. He was nervous and came unarmed and alone just as he was told. Although he knew that Louisa was safe at home, he would have to act as though her life depended on every word he spoke and every movement he made. He hoped that Erik's plan would work and that they would be rid of the two men forever.

As he neared the entrance to the cellars from the Rue Scribe he saw the two men coming toward him. He opened his coat, showing them that he had no pistol or other weapon concealed within his clothing. Danush pushed him forward, shoving a pistol into his back.

"Walk Daroga," Danush gruffly ordered.

They walked through the opening and then down into the caverns of the cellar. They traveled the ledge of the rat catcher and found themselves back at the place where they had thought Hessam had died the first time they had been there. This time they were able to climb down the metal ladder rungs to the bottom of the canal where only a foot of water stood. Hessam walked them to the torch holder and pulled it. The gate rose and allowed them entrance into the area where the lake shore reached the bottom of the bulkhead walls. They waded through the water that was now only ankle deep and then stopped on the shore.

"Where is the lake house and how do we enter?" Fardin asked.

Hessam replied with a question of his own, "Where is the girl?"

Danush pushed the pistol into his back harder this time and said, "She's in a safe place and as soon as you give us entry into the lake house and we find the Red Diamond we'll tell you where she is."

"How do I know that you haven't killed her already?"

"You don't but if you keep asking these questions you may find that you won't live to find her."

"Let's not play games now. I know that you've no intentions of letting me go. I will surely meet my death today. My only concern is what you will do with the girl."

"It is good that you have made your peace with meeting your death today. It will ease my conscience when I put the bullet through your skull." Danush laughed. "As for the girl, I will tell you where she is once you show me how to get into the lake house."

Hessam pointed at the staircase and said, "There is where you'll find entry into the lake house. Go to the second landing and push on the brick that is marked with an OG in its upper right hand corner. A door should present itself."

"You first," Danush said as he pushed Hessam toward the staircase.

They walked to the top of the second landing and Danush insisted that Hessam be the one to open the door. Danush and Fardin stood behind him on the landing as Hessam pushed on a brick that was in the wall which he knew wouldn't open a door, at least not in front of him. As he released the pressure from the wall the floor quickly dropped out from under the two men. Fardin fell completely in and Danush held fast to the edge and managed to take hold of Hessam's leg as he descended into the hole. Hessam fought to keep his balance and kicked Danush in the face sending him into the darkness. He then entered the lake house from the hidden door underneath the staircase.

The two men wound down the tubular chute with great speed and quickly landed in the chamber where the mirrors were already warm from the lights. Fardin was the first one to land in the room. He landed feet first but his landing was awkward and he was unbalanced which sent him backward hitting his head on the ground so forcefully that it knocked him unconscious. Danush followed and landed on top of Fardin. He pushed himself off of his colleague and then sat for a few minutes trying to get his bearings. Danush rose from the floor and began banging on the mirrors, hoping they would break. They didn't. Instead he burned his hands which angered him even more. He began screaming for Hessam to release them but it wasn't Hessam's voice that answered his plead.

"It is your own greed that has imprisoned you," a deep searing voice bellowed through the lake house. "You have come where you weren't invited. How dare you enter here?"

Danush boldly answered, "Who are you?"

The voice replied, "I wouldn't concern myself too much with who I am if I were you. I would be more concerned about what is going to happen to you and your friend. All you need to know is that death has already claimed my life and you shall surely join me there within a few hours unless you do as you are told."

Peter stood outside the room with Hessam as they listened to Erik taunt his victims. Erik stayed out of sight readying himself for what was about to occur.

Danush became frightened as the voice spoke to him. He knew that the voice could only belong to one person and that was the once assassin for the Shah.....Erik. Was it possible that his restless soul wandered the cellars protecting his home from being discovered? No, it couldn't be possible that the spirit of a madman was here taunting them, this was a trick.

Danush, although frightened spoke once again. "If you are a spirit then you will know why it is that I have come here. Tell me what it is I seek and I will believe that you aren't of this world."

Erik had missed the tricks and games and was very happy to oblige the man with an answer that even he didn't expect. "I won't only tell you why you have come, I will show you. Look into the mirror near the iron tree. There I will reveal to you your heart's desire."

At that moment the Red Diamond appeared in the tree. An obvious trick conjured by the use of mirrors but not realized by the man it was meant to persuade that he was indeed speaking with an apparition. Fardin had finally regained consciousness and watched as Danush tried unsuccessfully to retrieve the red gem."

"Why can't I hold it in my hand ghost?" Danush asked in a demanding tone.

Erik replied in a condescending tone, "I said I would show you your heart's desire, I never said I would give it to you." He waited for his prisoner to respond but there was only silence. Fardin was starting to strip away his clothing due to the rising temperature in the room. Danush continued to try to find a way out.

"Where is the Red Diamond?" a desperate and sweltering Danush screamed.

"It is in a room far from here; a room that you won't dare to ever enter as long as you live," the voice answered.

The heat in the room was becoming too much for Fardin and he grabbed Danush by the front of his shirt. He was soaked in sweat and he had a crazed look in his eyes. "Get us out of here before we die. Whatever the spirit wants us to do, promise him that we'll do it."

"You fool!" Danush snapped as he pushed Fardin to the floor. "It is no spirit that we are dealing with but the Opera Ghost himself....... Erik."

"But he is dead, Danush. I can see him. I can see him in the mirror but he is not in the room." Fardin pointed and there stood Erik, with one of his old masks affixed to his face and completely dressed in black.

Fardin was right, he wasn't actually in the room just as the Red Diamond wasn't either but the mirrors made it appear that he was. Danush dropped to his knees and began begging for mercy. The two were now convinced that it was a ghost to whom they were speaking. Erik could tell by their reactions and appearance that they were about to succumb to the torture chambers menacing attributes. His image as well as the Red Diamond's suddenly disappeared and he joined Hessam and Peter in the main room. He motioned for them to join him in the room that was once where he slept.

"Erik, how much longer are you going to allow this to go on?" Peter asked.

"Don't worry Peter. I'm not going to let them die."

"But what if they choose to use the lassos? How will you keep that from happening?"

"They can't use what is not there. I took them out last night. In fact, while you were resting peacefully I was busy revising my plans for these two gentlemen."

"I hope you intend on explaining yourself," Hessam stated with a slight agitation noted in his voice.

"Don't I always?" Erik said as he took a seat on the edge of his organ bench. "It occurred to me after I spoke to Peter last night that the only way to rid us of these two men without actually killing them is to give them what they want or something better."

Hessam and Peter gave each other a passing glance and then their eyes returned to Erik as he continued to elaborate on his plan.

"You see it is very simple. First I thought it best to return the two men to the Shah which would definitely clear our hands of having anything to do with their deaths. However, in doing so I realized that the Shah would see fit to execute them. I couldn't in good conscience send them to their deaths knowing that they were just as much a victim of the Shah's self-serving plans as I once had been. I don't wish for their lives to be ended just for them to leave us all alone."

Peter was becoming impatient and interrupted Erik. "Is there a point to all of this my friend?"

"Be patient Peter, I'm getting to the point." He walked over to a table and picked up a leather case, placing it in front of them. "I have twenty-five thousand francs in this leather case. Hessam will offer all of it to them and remain steadfast to his story that he doesn't have or know where the Red Diamond is. They can buy their passage to America and start their new lives there. In addition to offering them the money he will promise the two men that the Shah will never come looking for them."

"You can't be serious Erik? How are we going to keep that from happening?" Hessam argued.

"We are going to go to Persia and return the Red Diamond of Nadirijna to the Shah himself," Erik announced.

Hessam rubbed his chin and thought about what Erik was proposing. "I think I understand your plan. How do you presume to get back to Persia?" Hessam asked.

"I will secure passage on a small shipping vessel for two passengers from the Port of Marseille to the Port of Antalya from there we will board a train and make our way to Mazenderan. I need only one of you to come with me. I'll let the two of you decide who that will be."

Peter began to speak and then Hessam motioned to him to stay quiet. "I'll go with you Erik. I know the terrain better than he and this is our mess, not his."

"I agree. However, you realize the risk you're taking by returning to Persia. You were exiled and ordered never to return. It could cost you your freedom as well as your life," Erik reminded him.

"I realize that but you must also remember that we have something that the Shah wants."

Peter watched them as they discussed their plans and then interrupted them saying, "While the two of you are traveling the world what is it that I am to do?"

Erik put his arm around Peter's shoulder and said to him, "I'll need you, Darius and Chester to make sure our friends buy their tickets and get on the next ocean liner destined for America. Take them back to Hessam's flat if necessary until you can board a train to take them to a city near the port. Find ample lodging for all of you until their departure. I know I can count on all of you to make sure that they have left. After that is done all of you may return to Tri-Chateau. I need you to explain everything to Amalie and to give her this in the event that I don't return but *only* if I don't return." He handed Peter a sealed envelope.

"You're coming back Erik. Both of you are."

"I can't guarantee it but I am hoping the same too." Erik said as he put his hand on Peter's shoulder and looked in his eyes.

"What will you do once you get to Persia?" Peter asked.

"I have telegraphed your friend André asking him to meet us at the railway station in four days with some kind of transportation. If he doesn't show up then we'll have to secure transport for ourselves."

"That shouldn't be hard to do." Hessam said. "Money speaks all languages and quiets all tongues."

"Anyhow, once we get to Mazenderan I haven't quite figured out what to do," Erik said as he paced around the room. "My biggest concern was getting us there."

"I know what to do," said Hessam. "It will be risky but I believe that it's the best way to rid us of the Red Diamond and possibly gain the approval of the Shah." He planted himself in front of Erik and put his hands on his shoulders while looking him in the eyes. "You won't be able to come with me into the palace Erik. They will surely kill us both if you do."

"I'll be in the palace you just won't be able to see me. Have you forgotten that I built the edifice that is contrived of hidden doors and passageways? I will certainly be there making sure that all goes as planned."

Peter had ventured out of the room briefly to check on their visitors in the other room. There were no voices or noises at all coming from within the mirrored walls. Peter walked quickly back to where he had left Hessam and Erik planning their ruse.

"I think our visitors have succumbed to the heat gentlemen. I think it's time that we put our plans into actions," Peter announced.

Erik climbed to a platform where he could see inside the chamber and saw that they were soaked with perspiration and not moving. Then he tossed the key to Peter and told him to unlock the door. Peter and Hessam pulled the two men out, took their weapons, clothed them and then gagged and bound their hands and feet. They carried them to the shore of the lake, leaned them up against the bulkhead walls and waited for them to regain consciousness. Erik and Peter went back into the lair leaving Hessam to carry out the plan. He hoped that they would agree to it.

While inside the lair Erik took his sword from his waist and prepared his bag for his departure.

"Won't you need that?" asked Peter.

"No, it's the weapon of someone I no longer identify with and it is best to be buried here with all of the other things in my life that I no longer want or need," Erik said as he laid it next to the organ.

"I hope that these men will accept Hessam's offer."

"I hope so too Peter or I'm going to have to come up with a different plan," Erik laughed.

"I've told Hessam that I would meet him at the train station. Please be careful. Remember these two men are trained guards."

"I will and you do the same," Peter said as he shook Erik's hand and watched him leave through the secret door that led to the bakery. Peter exited the lair through the entrance under the stairs of the bulkhead and stayed there; waiting to hear if Danush and Fardin would agree to Hessam's offer.

Hessam had grown tired of waiting for the two men to awaken so he took a bucket, filled it with water and threw it on them. The coolness of the water made them wake slightly. He waited for a few more minutes and drew another bucket of water. He was about to toss it onto them and Danush began squirming and moaning. Hessam set the bucket down and knelt next to him.

"I will remove your gag if you promise not to scream. Do you promise?" Hessam asked.

Danush and Fardin, who had just woken fully, nodded in agreement. Hessam took their gags from their mouths. Danush was the first to speak.

"Why are we not in the lair?"

"I don't think that you're in a position to ask that question. I would think you would be thanking me for saving your lives."

"*You* saved our lives?" Fardin asked.

"Yes I did."

"Why would you do that?" Danush asked.

"Because what you seek you will never find. I don't know where it is and if Erik knew where it was he has taken that secret to his grave. However, I know that you won't believe me so I have a proposition for the two of you."

"And just exactly what would that be?"

"I have in this leather case twenty-five thousand francs. It is yours if you'll agree to arrange passage to America on the next ocean liner that is leaving France. My colleagues and I will personally escort you to the ship and see you off on your voyage. In return you will never seek to harm me or my friends and their families again."

"Why would we accept your offer when the Shah has promised us much more for the return of the gem?" Danush arrogantly asked.

"Because I know he never sent you to look for it and I also know that the Shah is now looking for the two of you. You stole a gem that all of you believed to be the Red Diamond of Nadirijna for him. He asked you to replace it with a gem that looked like the real one so that he could later pretend to wear the real Red Diamond without being affected by the ancient curse. Then after you found out it wasn't the real Red Diamond you came looking for me believing that I might know where the real Red Diamond was being kept. Does any of this sound familiar?" Hessam smugly commented. "You see, I know that the Shah will put you both to death if he ever finds you. So, I would think that my offer is rather reasonable, don't you?"

Fardin looked at Danush and then quickly answered, "Yes, I agree. We'll do as you ask." Danush gave him a disapproving look and then said, "Silence you fool. Let me handle this. Although your offer is tempting what will keep you from alerting the Shah of our whereabouts?"

"Your memory is short Danush. I was exiled from Persia by the Shah so why would he believe anything that I have to say?

Danush still didn't trust the Daroga and was working unsuccessfully to free himself from his bondage while he continued to ask questions. "What will you do with us if we refuse your offer?"

"I suppose I have no other choice but to put you back into the chamber from which I saved you and let you die."

Fardin was desperate now and began pleading with Danush. "Please sir, accept the offer. I can't go back into that room of invisible fire. I would rather take a pistol to my temple than return to that nightmare. The spirits face will haunt me as well as his voice."

Danush looked at his weak companion and knew that if he didn't accept the offer Fardin would and then he would be put back into the mirrored room alone to die.

"What guarantees will I have that you won't come looking for us?" Danush asked.

"Like you, I carried out many plans of a shah who thought only of himself. I can only assume that although you may have thought his request deceitful you did what he asked because you had no other choice. I'm sure he promised you many things as well which he never intended to give you. And how do I know this? I know because he did, after all send Fardin to kill you." Hessam turned to Fardin as he paced up and down the shore of the lake. "And Fardin, what do you think he was going to do with you when you returned with Danush's body?"

Fardin sat quietly pondering what his fate would have been but never spoke. Hessam then answered his own question. "I'll tell you what he would've done.....he would have killed you as well. All of his servants are disposable to him and that is why I don't wish you harmed. I refuse to act or think like him. I have more regard for a man's life."

"You haven't inquired about the girl, Daroga? What if I tell you that the girl will surely die if you don't set us free and give us the Red

Diamond?" Danush posed his question in hopes that it would persuade Hessam to let them go.

"I would say that you are mistaken. I know that the girl has escaped and she is no longer in your possession."

Danush and Fardin looked at each other with surprise crossing their faces. How could he know this? What magic was this man conjuring to know what had happened to the girl?

"How is it that you know she is not with us?" Danush asked angrily; his plans now completely in shambles.

"I have many more friends than the two of you and that is all I'll say on the matter. Now, I must compel you both to give me your answer. The hour is late and our transportation will be arriving soon."

Fardin looked at Danush and with his eyes told him that it was best to take the money and start a new life. Danush looked at Hessam and said, "We have an agreement. We will go with you and arrange to leave France.....forever."

"Very well, I will untie your feet so that you may walk but your hands will remain bound until we reach our destination. I hope you'll forgive me but I don't trust you not to try to get away."

"It's understood Daroga. I don't trust you either," Danush said.

Just then Peter made his presence known to Hessam and began helping him untie the men. "Let's go before we worry Darius and Chester. I'm sure they are anxious to know what has happened."

Peter climbed out of the opening that opened up to the Rue Scribe and walked back and forth searching for Chester and Darius. It was only a few minutes until they arrived. Peter helped their guests into the coach and joined them inside. Darius mounted Jasper and Chester stayed atop the coach as driver. Hessam boarded the wagon, leaving to meet Erik at the train station. Peter told Darius to lead them to Hessam's flat.

When they reached the flat, Peter told Chester and Darius individually of Erik's new plans and what they were to do. Chester was not at all happy about his son leaving but he was proud of him for making a decision that reflected his beliefs. He had changed and God had provided him a way to keep his promise which was not to return to the ways of the man he once was. He had hoped that this nightmare would be over by now but knew that it was just beginning for his son. He went to the bedroom, took his Bible from his bag and began reading. After he had read for a while he set it on the night stand and then prayed to God; asking him to keep Erik and Hessam safe.

Faithful Servant

When they arrived at the railway station in the province of Hyrcania it was almost dawn. Erik readied himself to exit the train before Hessam. As Erik left the passenger car where they had been he searched the station for a man that fit André's description. There was no one there. He knew that it was probable that he wouldn't be there for many reasons other than the obvious. He searched for someone from whom he could possibly rent two horses. He approached a man that was customarily dressed but upon seeing his face realized that he wasn't Persian. The man stepped back at the sight of Erik's mask and then proceeded politely to speak to him with a French accent. Upon hearing his voice Erik knew that this was Peter's friend André.

"Sir, are you by chance acquainted with a man from France?" Erik whispered.

"Yes I am and you are welcome to my horses and wagon sir but I shall not journey with you. I can't risk being seen with you as I am partial to keeping my head."

"I appreciate your honesty and it is quite all right. I think that we'll be able to handle it from here. I may not be able to return your horses or wagon sir. Please, take this in return for your trouble." Erik took out several hundred francs and placed them in his hand.

"Thank you sir, you're quite generous. Whatever I don't use I will find a way to get back to you. Please sir, be quick and don't linger. Few eyes see all things."

André disappeared into the crowd before Erik was even able to thank him. He pulled his cloak collar up higher so that no one would know he was wearing a mask, climbed onto the wagon and met his friend at the station. Hessam climbed onto the wagon and then they traveled throughout the city, stopping only once at an outdoor café for something to eat.

When they reached the area near the palace, Erik unhitched the horses abandoning the wagon. They each took a horse and climbed atop. Erik handed Hessam the Red Diamond of Nadirijna that was still in the black pouch and gave him a look of confidence. They parted ways and Erik headed for the tunnel which would lead him into the treasury room and give him access into the palace. Erik wasn't worried that the door may be locked because he was a master at opening locked doors without keys. Although he believed that the doors wouldn't be guarded he would proceed with caution.

When he reached the door of the treasury room he turned the knobs hoping that it was unlocked. It wasn't. He used his skills and released the lock. He then took his sgian-dhu from his boot readying himself for the possibility of encountering a guard. He slowly opened the door and looked around. There was no one directly in his path but he could hear several guards talking which meant they were making their rounds and reporting back to their superior. He waited until he thought that they had moved in a direction that he wasn't going and moved out of the treasury room. Unfortunately, one of the guards had decided to come back to the hall where Erik was. Erik quickly went back into the treasury room hiding against the wall beside the door. This way if the door was opened he would be hidden by it when it was opened.

Erik could hear the guard's footsteps as he walked by the room. Then he heard the handle of the door turn. The door opened and the guard entered with his weapon drawn. Erik stood very still hoping that the guard wouldn't question the door being open. This didn't happen. He moved into the room to turn on the lights. When the lights illuminated the room, he saw that nothing in the room was disturbed. The guard scratched his head and then turned quickly, thinking that someone was behind him. When he looked he saw no one. Then he slowly approached the door, grabbed the knob and then looked behind it. No one was there. While the guard had walked to turn on the lights Erik had slipped quietly out of the room and down the hall into a room that would give him entry into the internal secret passages of the palace. The guard turned out the lights and secured the room before resuming his patrol.

Hessam rode up to the palace gates and was met by four guards. Two stood beside him and the other two stood in front of the gate.

"Who are you and what are you selling today?" one of the guards asked.

"I am the former Daroga of Mazenderan who the Shah exiled many years ago. I am not a seller of fine rugs or any other items; I'm merely returning to him that which is his."

"I don't know of anything that he has lost sir. All that he wants or needs is already in his possession."

"Give me an audience with his majesty so that I may show him that I'm still his faithful and dutiful servant," Hessam begged.

The head of the Royal Guard heard the commotion and walked over to see what he thought was an altercation that his men couldn't handle. When he looked to see who the person was causing the problems he recognized him immediately. He pulled him down off of the horse and bound his hands.

"Bring the horse," the head guard said as he thrust Hessam in front of him.

Two of the men took charge of the horse and the others followed them into the court. As the head guard brought Hessam forward everyone in the court was whispering and pointing. They recognized who Hessam was and wondered why he had returned. When they reached the inner court where the Shah was perched on his throne, the guard bowed and so did Hessam.

The Shah rose to his feet, walked to where Hessam stood and looked him up and down. Then he motioned one of the guards to cut the bindings from his hands.

"You were not wise to have come back here Daroga! However, it intrigues me that you would risk your life to come here. What is it that makes you do such a thing? Tell me Daroga."

"I have with me something that I believe you have been searching for these past months."

The Shah was surprised by what his former protector had just announced.

"You've gotten my attention Daroga. What is it that you have found that you believe that I have been searching for these past months?"

"Your majesty, I recovered your gem and apprehended the two men that stole it and that is why I have returned to Persia at the risk of you taking my life."

"What gem Daroga?"

"Why the Red Diamond of Nadirijna."

The men standing in the court began to whisper again. This time it was not whispers of wonder but of suspicion as to why this man was claiming to have a jewel that was supposedly adorning the head of their Shah at this very moment.

"But that is impossible the Red Diamond of Nadirijna has been affixed to my turban for months. How can you return something that was never lost?" The Shah could hear the whispers growing louder, this time they seemed angry. He knew that soon he would be found out and he would have to take matters into his own hands to save himself.

What he was about to find out was that his faithful servant was soon to rescue him.

"If it was never lost then how do you explain this?"

Hessam reached into his shirt and pulled out the small black pouch, untied the leather strap and poured the gem into his hands. The crowd gasped as he held it in his fingers showing it around the room to all that could see it. "Here is your gem sir and you are quite right, it *isn't* the Red Diamond of Nadirijna, it is a clever imposter that the two men that stole it tried to pass off as such to a jeweler."

Hessam could see the tension from the Shah's face drain like a bucket of spilled milk with this revelation about the gem.

"Of course it's not the Red Diamond of Nadirijna. How could it be? It's been here on my turban all of this time."

"Exactly your majesty and I knew this. Yet when I asked these two men how they had come to be in possession of this particular gem, they ranted on like mad men speaking of how you had asked them to steal it but once they had taken it they found it to be an imposter, not the Red Diamond. I can honestly say that I believe these two men to have gone mad. I, of course, would never believe that such treachery would have been ordered by you so I had to assume that they had acted on their own. Then they began ranting that the contriver of your palace had stolen the real Red Diamond of Nadirijna years ago. Nothing they said made sense. I have no idea what had befallen them on their journey but it must have been terrible to have broken their minds like it did."

Erik was now listening inside the walls where the passageways he had erected many years ago hid him. He was impressed with Hessam's performance and was optimistic that soon this event would be over; hopefully without incident.

The Shah stood in front of Hessam silent for several minutes holding the red gem in his hands. The Shah wanted the gem because he believed it was the actual Red Diamond of Nadirijna however, he also knew that by the way Hessam looked at him that Hessam knew it too and yet he didn't expose his deception to the people of Persia. Unexpected was the kindness of a man that he had exiled from his home so long ago. He didn't understand the reasons behind Hessam's generosity. Why wouldn't he have kept it for himself? He would soon get his answers but for now he had to find a way to make sure that no one in his court thought twice about what Hessam claimed that Danush and Fardin had accused the Shah of asking them to do. He knew what he had to do. He would offer it to the Daroga. Offering it to him would dispel any suspicion that the gem was truly the Red Diamond and if Hessam accepted it, he could easily get it back.

"Daroga, put out your hand," the Shah said loudly so that all could hear him.

Hessam put his hand out and in it the Shah laid the gem that Hessam had taken from the bag earlier. "I have many gems and treasures but none are as valuable as a good and faithful servant. Even at the risk of losing your own life you chose to remain a loyal servant of Persia. As a gesture of my appreciation and thanks for returning what is mine, I give you the gem which they took from me and you are no longer exiled from the lands of Persia. From this day forth you are welcome once again in the country of your birth."

"I'm humbled by your generosity your majesty. I cannot in good conscience accept a treasure that belongs to the people of Persia however, I will accept the pardon you have granted me and I shall consider the matter closed."

The Shah was relieved because now he wouldn't have to ever worry about anyone finding out that the Red Diamond he wore was not real at all. He would always have the authentic gem to prove it had never been missing.

"Again you have shown your loyalty to not only me but to the people you served for many years. Please join me in my private chambers for something to eat and drink. I'm sure that your journey has given you an appetite for something more than adventure," the Shah said as he walked in front of Hessam leading him into his private chambers. Once they reached the interior of the room the Shah motioned for his guards to leave them. He had something important to discuss with the man who seemed to be more forgiving than what the Shah thought he should be.

"I'm not going to waste my time with idle chatter Daroga. Instead I'll get straight to the point. Let us not pretend that you don't believe what has transpired between me and the two men. You know that the gem you have returned is the actual Red Diamond of Nadirijna. What puzzles me is why you haven't exposed my secret. Tell me, Daroga, why do you feel the need to protect me?"

"You showed me mercy once did you not? I am only returning the favor."

"You mentioned that the two men thought that Erik had taken off with the Red Diamond of Nadirijna. Why would they believe that Erik had the real Red Diamond when they knew that the gem they had in their possession was the actual Red Diamond of Nadirijna which I paid them to steal and replace with a cleverly disguised ruby?" the Shah said as he sat down on an ornate chair that sat behind a large desk.

"Perhaps it is because they wished me to believe that the gem they had wasn't the genuine Red Diamond so that I wouldn't return them to you. People say and do strange things when they are trying to save their own lives."

"I would say you're assumptions are probably correct. May I ask what has happened to the two men?"

"Sadly they are no longer of any consequence to you or I sir. They resisted my authority when I was trying to bring them back to you and I had no choice but to kill both of them. Their bodies are now at the bottom of the sea."

Hessam looked in the Shah's eyes to see if he believed him. He knew that it was possible that he wouldn't since he had lied to him about Erik all those years ago.

"I see," the Shah said as he paced the floor. "That leaves me to wonder what it is that you wish to gain from knowing this secret that you and I only know. Someone doesn't give up something so valuable without wanting something in return."

"I only wished to return to you what was yours your majesty. I had hoped that it would show you that I was truly sorry for what happened all those years ago. Your favor was all I sought and I would say that I have gained that since you have granted me a pardon. I wish only to return to my home and live out my days in peace and tranquility. You now have your Red Diamond of Nadirijna back where it belongs and if anyone ever questions the authenticity of the one you wear you will be able to present this one and no one will ever know that you have been deceiving them."

"After all that I have put you through Daroga, you show me mercy and kindness. Why?"

"That was years ago sir and had I been in your position I would've done what you did. You are the Shah and you have to act as such. Sometimes your decisions are not easy to make. I never held any ill will toward you sir. Instead I was grateful that you spared my life. It is only right that I show you the same mercy."

"What is to keep you from telling someone else what you know?"

"What good would it do when you can prove me wrong your majesty? You have the Red Diamond of Nadirijna. Besides I have just announced in your court that I didn't believe such treachery. If I recanted then I would be a liar and they would surely know that I was trying to take advantage of you."

Erik listened as his friend worked to put the Shah's mind at ease. A reasonable man would have accepted the words that Hessam spoke but the Shah was not such a man. His fear of exposure was what was driving him. The tension in the room began to grow as the Shah became more and more nervous. Erik feared that his assistance might be needed soon.

"Daroga, I'm inclined to believe you but as a man in my position it is hardly reasonable to believe that you would never tell anyone my secret. Therefore, I must see to it that you never speak a word of this to anyone."

"How will you justify killing me as a traitor when everyone in that room believes me to be otherwise?" Hessam nervously asked as he began moving away from the Shah.

"I will tell them that you tried to take my life and steal the Red Diamond from me."

"But I have no weapon sir. How will you explain that?"

"I'm the Shah and I don't have to explain anything! I do as I please."

He drew his saber and Hessam began moving more quickly toward the wall where he knew there was a secret door. It was good that Erik had divulged the locations of the secret exits in each room to him. He truly didn't believe he would have a need to access them but Erik insisted he memorize them just in case. The Shah drew his saber up ready to swing and then a blast of red and orange smoke that then turned to darkness enveloped the room. Erik grabbed Hessam and pulled him into the secret door. They ran quickly through the passageways and then exited into the hall outside the treasury room. Erik looked around making sure there was no one around and then he unlocked the doors once again. They entered the large empty room bringing the doors shut behind them. Erik raised the trap door in the floor and then they exited the room entering the tunnel that would take them to their freedom.

The Shah who was still coughing and blinded by the smoke was surprised. After the smoke cleared he looked around to see where his victim was and he was nowhere to be found. He couldn't possibly have gotten out of the room without him seeing him and he couldn't have gone past the guards that were outside the room. The guards heard the Shah coughing and came running into the room.

"Are you all right your majesty?"

"Yes, I'm fine."

"Where is the daroga?"

"He has obviously left. Didn't he go out through the doors?" The guards looked at each other in amazement. They never saw him leave.

"How do you mean your majesty? We didn't see him exit."

"Then where is he?" asked the Shah angrily.

"I don't know sir but we'll find him!" one of the guards said.

Just then the Shah's advisor entered the room. The look on his face was one of bewilderment.

"Why is your sword drawn your majesty?"

"The daroga tried to attack me and take back the gem."

"Why would he do that when you had already offered it to him and he refused it?"

"Why do you dare question me Mahtab?"

"I'll not apologize for questioning what I do not understand. I am here to advise you on important matters and if you repeat this accusation against the man who has brought back what is yours, I believe that everyone will question it as I do. So I will ask you again, why is your sword drawn?"

The Shah knew that he couldn't reveal his secret to yet another person and he also knew that Mahtab was correct to assume that everyone else would question his accusation if he did in fact continue with it. He had to think of something and quickly. He knew now that no one would ever believe that the daroga was of any consequence to him after his courageous deed.

"I'm quite embarrassed Mahtab. The Daroga was showing me a magic trick he learned on one of his travels. I was startled when it erupted and it was my instinct to pull my sword. He said that he would disappear but I didn't believe him. Obviously his magic worked since I have no idea where he has gone."

Mahtab didn't believe this story entirely either but it did explain the smoke and it was more believable than the Daroga attacking him when he had no weapon.

"Your majesty, I believe it is just as well that he left without being seen. His presence has made many people anxious. Did he say what he hoped to gain from coming here?"

"Only that he wished to return what was mine and to return to his home to live out his days in peace. His returning the gem was a gift for my sparing his life many years ago."

"I would say that he has fully paid his debt to you sir and I hope that his wish of returning home, wherever that is, will be fulfilled." Mahtab replied.

"I'm sure it will be. Tell the guards to stop searching for him and if they do cross paths with him to let him go."

Mahtab nodded acknowledging the Shah's orders. He left the room leaving the Shah alone. The Shah put his sword away and then after looking around the room to make sure that no one would see him, he opened the secret door. He knew that this was how Hessam had left. Unfortunately, he couldn't risk involving anyone else in the secret that he shared only with the Daroga. He would have to trust that he wouldn't share the knowledge he had with anyone else. He truly had no other choice. However, he didn't have to worry about his lie being discovered by those around him. He would finally rest knowing that the Red Diamond of Nadirijna was back in his possession.

As Erik and Hessam neared the end of the tunnel they were out of breath and breathing hard.

"And you thought you wouldn't need to know the secrets of the palace," Erik said to Hessam.

"Yes and you believed that the Shah would just let me walk out without any resistance even though I knew his secret," Hessam said as he rolled his eyes at his naïve friend.

"I never said I *thought* he would, I said that I *hoped* he would. There's a difference, you know."

"Well, you were wrong on both accounts no matter how you word it. I was lucky to escape with my life."

"You were never in any danger. I was always prepared to come to your aid."

"But I had no idea that you had made it into the palace at all."

"I'm disappointed that you would doubt my capabilities."

"Well, you're not as young as you once were Erik and neither am I for that matter."

"It is true that we're older now but youth has no advantage over intelligence and I would say that we've outsmarted our adversary once again. Besides he's not as young as he once was either."

Hessam looked at Erik and smiled. They both began to laugh as they made their way to Erik's horse. Erik climbed on and then pulled Hessam up to take a seat behind him. They rode back to the station where no one questioned or stopped them. It appeared that they had indeed rid themselves of the Red Diamond of Nadirijna.

The Rarest Gem

*A*malie had anxiously waited for more than a week for the return of Erik and Hessam. As each day passed with no word from them she worried that something went terribly wrong and she had to prepare herself for that possibility. Losing him would be even harder than losing her father and mother. It would be as if a part of her own soul had been taken from her and how would she explain to Louisa why her father hadn't returned. That would be the worse part of them not coming home. She couldn't think about that right now, she needed to focus on making breakfast. Louisa would be up soon and the others would also be arriving. She had asked that they all come for breakfast every morning until Erik and Hessam were safely at home. It started her day in a positive way and although the others may have thought it was a silly request they never denied her. This was the eleventh day that they would come to the house for breakfast and every day they all hoped that it would be the last time they had to come under these circumstances.

Amalie had finished cooking the bacon and had started cooking the eggs when she heard a scratch at the back door. She stopped what she was doing and went to the back door. She knew it had to be Sampson. His nose was trained to smell the bacon like a hunting dog could sniff out a fox. She opened the door and there he sat looking at her with his big green eyes. This particular morning, he had brought her a gift but it wasn't the usual dead rodent he liked to bring her, instead between his feet was a small black pouch.

"Well, what do we have here Sampson? This is much better than what you usually bring me. Go on in, your milk is in the bowl and I'll get your bacon soon." She pushed him gently into the house. She knelt down, picked up the pouch and opened it. In it was a note that read:

Amalie,
You are still the rarest gem of us all.
Hessam

She could feel that there was something in the bottom of the pouch and she pushed her fingers down into it to retrieve it. She felt something hard and then pulled it out. It was a red gemstone. She looked outside to see where it had come from or who might have put it there. No one was there. When she turned to go back into the house Erik was standing in the kitchen looking at her and Hessam was beside him.

Amalie began to cry and then ran into his arms. She kissed him passionately on the lips and didn't care that Hessam was watching.

"Thank God you are safe, both of you."

"We're glad to be home. It was an adventure neither of us ever care to repeat."

"Come in and sit. Let me take your coats and gloves. There is hot water for tea on the stove. Please help yourselves to anything you wish," Amalie said as she gathered their things and walked out of the room to put them into the closet.

Sampson had finished his milk and was in search of someone to feed him his bacon. He rubbed his body against Erik's boot and began purring loudly. Erik felt the vibration of his purr and bent down from his chair to pet him.

"I missed you too old fellow but I'm afraid you'll have to wait for Amalie to feed you. I haven't the energy Sampson. I know you understand," he said as he continued to pet him.

Sampson continued to purr and then as Amalie entered the room he left Erik's side and followed her over to the plate where the bacon was sitting on the counter. She gave him a crumbled piece of bacon on a saucer and then wiped her hands on a towel to rid them of the grease. She took the pouch with the red jewel in it out of her apron pocket and placed it on the table in front of Hessam.

"As happy as I am to see the two of you, I would like to know why this has made its way back to our house."

Her searing disapproving gaze was fixed upon Erik.

"Don't ask me, this is the first time that I have seen it since I gave it to Hessam to return to the Shah. I thought he was just using the pouch to send you a note. I had no idea that there was anything inside of it," Erik said as he glared at Hessam with disapproval. "I saw you give it to the Shah and I saw him put it inside his vest. How is it that you have it?"

They waited for Hessam to explain as he sat in silence gathering his thoughts. Amalie continued cooking the eggs knowing that she could no longer delay preparing breakfast since everyone would be there shortly. In the meantime, Erik was growing impatient and angry.

"I'm waiting Hessam. I specifically told you to give it back to him. Why would you do this? Why would you put us all in danger again?"

Hessam rose from his chair and walked over to Sampson. He picked him up and stroked his fur as he walked around the room. "I never had any intentions of giving it to him Erik. That was your plan, not mine."

"Why?"

"Isn't it obvious to you that our Shah has used many people to better his own station in life? You and I were two of those people. He never worried about what happened to us or the hundreds, possibly thousands that he has put to death in order to hide his secrets."

"Is this truly the Red Diamond of Nadirijna that is on my table?" Amalie angrily asked.

"Yes it is."

"Then what is it that the Shah is now passing off as his precious rare gem?" Erik asked while he took a sip of the tea Amalie had brought him.

"It is a ruby that I had asked Peter to purchase for me before I left for Paris. Amalie had given me the real Red Diamond to give back to the Shah. She said that you had asked her to give it to me so that I could bring it to you but instead I had Peter take it so that he could buy a gem that was the approximate size and color to hand to you when he came to the flat. Amalie didn't send him with the gem, just the key. While you were giving us your theory as to what you thought had happened between the Shah and the two men, Peter slipped the real Red Diamond of Nadirijna into my hand when he greeted me before he took his seat."

"The two of you made your own plans without me. I should be disappointed but quite frankly I'm not. In fact I'm impressed that you took the initiative to do something about it yourself. I have only one question for you though. What is it that you hoped to have accomplished by not giving the real Red Diamond to him?"

"I don't honestly have to explain it to you, do I?" Hessam replied.

"It's probably because I'm tired and much older than I once was but yes, Hessam, I require you to explain it to me," Erik said with levity in his voice.

"I'll humor you because you saved my life again." Hessam took a seat at the table after putting Sampson back on the floor. "It's quite simple. I knew that he would never let me walk out of his palace alive once he knew that I was privy to all that he had done. I had actually thought about handing him the real Red Diamond at first but after I looked in his eyes while he spoke to me, all I could see was the selfish, heartless man that put thousands of workers to death for the sake of a few secret passageways. It turned my stomach. Then when he offered the ruby to me I thought about taking it but I knew that if I had he would have certainly come after me later to find it. This way, everyone saw that I let him keep it."

Erik was now more confused than when he had begun. "But no one in that room knows that it was supposed to be the real Red Diamond but you and the Shah." Erik interrupted. "So the reality Hessam is that all they think he owns is a ruby, which is exactly what you gave him."

"And that is exactly why it was the perfect solution. The Shah has no need to come looking for me or anyone else. *He* believes he has the Red Diamond of Nadirijna that's all that matters. He will store it away in a safe place where he can access it if by chance he ever needs to prove the one he has on his turban is authentic. When that day comes, neither of the gems will be the Red Diamond and who will they blame? It will not be me because I gave him a ruby and all were witness to it. He will be the one that will have to explain how the Red Diamond that he wore on his head daily disappeared without his knowledge or without a trace."

"You're brilliant my friend," Erik said as he clapped in approval and adoration. "I couldn't have thought of a better ending to his reign. Let's hope that he has a need to prove it soon." He laughed as he put his hand on Hessam's shoulder.

"What will you do with the Red Diamond until then?" asked Amalie as she poured Hessam a cup of tea.

"It is yours Amalie. That's why I gave it back to you. I have no use for such a jewel and you *are* by far the rarest gem of them all."

"I can't possibly accept it Hessam. It's an heirloom that belongs to you and your ancestors. You should give it to someone in your family."

Hessam rose from the table and walked over to Amalie with the pouch in his hand. He took her hands in his and placed the pouch in them. "I am giving it to someone in my family Amalie. You, Erik, Louisa, Darius and the rest of the people in this family are my family too. All of you have never treated me as anything different. So please take this gift. Have it made into a beautiful necklace or pendant. It's yours now."

Amalie's eyes watered at the tenderness of his words. She took it from his hands and then hugged him.

"Thank you Hessam. I will cherish it always."

Just then Louisa came running into the kitchen. Erik turned to face her as she came running up to him. He caught her in his arms and hugged her tightly.

"Father, you're home. I've been waiting forever for you to come back."

"I'm sure you have my angel. You'll wait no more because I'm never going to be gone for that long again. And if I am you'll both be coming with me; you and your mother."

He kissed her on the cheek and then put her down on the floor. "Help your mother get breakfast on the table."

"Yes Father," she said as she bounded through the kitchen collecting the plates to set the table.

The house filled with laughter and conversations as Chester, Meg, Yvette, Luc, Peter, Isabel and their daughters, Bella and Chloe all arrived for breakfast. Chester hugged Erik and Hessam. He was glad that nothing bad had happened to either of them. They all sat around the dining room table and Chester blessed the food and thanked God for the safe return of their loved ones. It was good to have everyone together; safe and sound.

After breakfast Amalie asked that Erik and Hessam speak with her in the drawing room while everyone else stayed in the great room visiting. Erik stood in front of her with his hands on her arms. "You look troubled Amalie. What is it?"

"Hessam has bestowed upon me this wonderful gem and although it seems to have brought some troubles our way, I know that it isn't the gem that has caused them. It is the evil deeds of men that cause such a beautiful thing to be looked upon with such contempt. Nevertheless I don't think that I can keep it. It really belongs with Hessam's family."

"Is this what you called us in here to tell us?" Hessam said while he laughed.

"Yes, it is. I know it sounds silly but it's the way I feel."

"Amalie, you have been like a sister to me and at times my guardian angel. You, Erik and Darius are all the family I have left and honestly I think that you're the only one that understands the true value of the gem." Hessam said to her as he lit a cigar.

Erik put his arms around her, kissing her tenderly on the forehead. "I agree with Hessam."

She was quiet for a moment while she thought about all of the things this gem had once been a part of since the day it had been taken from the Emperor of India until now. The people that had sought it were wicked and self-serving and now she was to be its owner. She kissed Erik on the cheek and squeezed Hessam on his forearm. She pulled out the gem and looked at it as it lay in her hand. She looked at both of them knowing how much they had both gone through in their lives in order to stay alive and protect their friendship. Their friendship was one that was as unlikely as that of her father's and Chester's; based on the heart of a person not social status or appearances. Their time together had made them more than just friends; they were family. She felt the same way. She knew that giving it back to him would be considered an insult but before she accepted it without reservations she wanted him to know how she felt about his gift. "It was this diamond that was given as a gift from you,' she looked at Erik, 'whose life was saved by you," she looked at Hessam. She looked at Hessam very humbled and with tears in her eyes and with a quivering voice she continued. "Now you believe that I am rarer than the gem itself just for loving Erik. However, Hessam, had you not saved him I wouldn't have had anyone to love. So it is you I believe to be the rarest of gems. I will accept this gift because I know the love in which it is being given however, you saw his worth first." She kissed Hessam on the cheek and smiled at him. "I know that I'm not worthy of your praises but I am blessed and humbled to have them. I'll do my best to honor them. This red diamond, although believed to have been cursed is not. It only needed to have love not hate as the reason for it being given or taken."

Erik kissed her on the forehead. "I couldn't agree with you more."

Amalie put the red diamond back into the pouch and handed it to Erik. He put it in his coat pocket and they joined the others in the great room.

LaVergne, TN USA
23 March 2011
221254LV00004B/77/P